CW01083634

Star Born

Eric Mackay

Grosvenor House
Publishing Limited

This book is published by
Grosvenor House Publishing Ltd
Link House
140 The Broadway, Tolworth, Surrey, KT6 7HT.
www.grosvenorhousepublishing.co.uk

This book is a work of fiction. Any resemblance to
people or events, past or present, is purely coincidental.

A CIP record for this book
is available from the British Library

ISBN 978-1-83615-204-0

This book is dedicated to Jean

Contents

Chapter 1   Material Matters   1

Chapter 2   Evolution Turns   15

Chapter 3   Dark   31

Chapter 4   Light   49

Chapter 5   Star Cult   75

Chapter 6   Stone of Destiny 107

Chapter 7   Orkney   141

Chapter 8   Battle   169

Chapter 9   Star Born   197

Chapter 10   Betrayal   241

Chapter 11   The Shadow   305

Contents

Introduction

The reader is introduced to our world in terminal societal decline. Then it is plunged into climate Armageddon, taking you into a primitive new world where survival is all.

Two enigmatic, mysterious others form opposing cults in what remains of a heat ravaged Scotland. Penumbra, the Star Bringer, for the dark and the pernicious Shadow and Aether, the Unicorn Queen, for the light and goodness.

Into this conflagration comes Airna, the Star Born, fighting for the light. Culminating in a battle of galactic dimensions where Airna pulls down her powers through the ancient neolithic standing stones of the Ring of Brodgar in Orkney and the star Arcturus.

Airna's quest is to eradicate the Shadow, used by the Watchers as a means of control for their promotion of evil and to feed their endless craving for the dark.

The cover of this novel is
an extract of a painting titled
"My Land" by the author

Chapter 1
Material Matters

It was 2115 and Max was entering old age, reflecting on the great adventure he had undertaken to establish a bright new world, absent of Shadows. He stretched and stared down at his right hand. The suggestion was still there. A faint but pervasive imprint of a unicorn. Max shivered. If only he, and others, had been saved all the pain and realised fully, just how precious goodness is and how easily it can fall.

Nobody saw what was coming. Even the rumour-mongers on the old world wide web, who had speculated extensively on all and every possible conspiracy theory, didn't see anything remotely like this coming. Science fiction writers had not come close to realising the extent and dimension of what transpired.

Many had postulated what level temperatures would reach and when, together with the expected social and economic ramifications. All forecasts were wrong and sorely underestimated the speed and ferocity of climate change.

In the 2020s social and economic issues were fiercely debated, with everyone having a point of view disseminated through multiple technical devices available for constant renewal and updating.

A dependency culture was created and commercialisation thrived with world populations progressively at the behest of technical companies. Key individuals and companies progressively set the broad world agenda rather than individual governments and institutions.

Manipulated by shopping algorithms, bombarded by bland addictive television, lives were being flattened. No system endures forever. Printing presses overturned the old feudal order and new technology overturned that which replaced it.

Polarised and aggressive consideration of often complex and controversial issues thrived, lacking both reason and logic. Reality became fiction and facts became lies. A great deal of confected anxiety and shock poured forth through multiple media outlets undermining the sensitive and vulnerable and mental health problems soared.

The inexorable rise of artificial capable intelligence brought about the end of human-dominated history, producing information, ideas and decisions independently and placed the crucial levers of control and power into alien, non-human, intelligence. Sadly, and as feared by many, the do-no-harm precautionary principles set to contain and regulate the capacity of artificial intelligence models faltered and fell in the face of the generation of more and more attractive new ideas, practices and concepts.

Despite this destabilising diet, there were, in day-to-day living, myriad examples of good news and goodness. It was all around and it mattered. You just never heard about it much in the news pumped out on a twenty-four-hour meat grinding cycle, relentlessly promoting and, complicity, valuing abnormal human behaviour. Any dialogue became negotiated self-interest. Many missed or were wilfully diverted from the good things that were outside the spotlight.

A further disturbing aspect of the utilisation of technology was the relentless introduction of surveillance. Not least, the progressive dehumanisation by Governments through the use of social credits awarded to those who behaved in stipulated ways that were rewarded with social advancement. Thereby shaping and modelling behaviour, confining it to preset norms and controlling what people did.

All this facilitated and maximised through a growing dependence on technology and an all-consuming addiction to our beloved screens. Goodness is unremarkable because it is the norm. The unstinting onslaught of the abnormal was like a malignant cancer feeding on the body of goodness.

A shallow, superficial world developed. Indeed, potentially one where most decisions were made by machines that had no concept of what it means to lead a meaningful and good life. Not all succumbed to digital pathogens but memetics were now all set to replace genetics. Artificial intelligence was on the move, eroding human creativity.

Warfare had succumbed to the pull of the unknown at the altar of humanity's ambition.

Gradually and relentlessly, minority views were promoted online and through the media. Social norms changed. Faith in government hit a new low and populations turned to their own agendas as to what was needed to get what they wanted. All of this was further facilitated by a growing adherence to belief systems which, for the most part, were in a constant state of conflict. All were convinced they were right and good and what they adhered to was right and good for everyone else.

Trust in institutions stuttered and the cult of the individual was stealthily promoted. The age of the sovereign individual had arrived. Those with phenomenal wealth moved out of the confines of their businesses and into government. Not as elected representatives but to fulfil their own agendas.

The one per cent became steadily richer. The old world was spinning in ever faster geopolitical motion threatening the rules based order that had yielded, since the second old world war, a five hundred per cent increase in living standards, increased longevity by ten years and had seen child mortality plummet.

Deciding, on global terms, what was wise or unwise, progressive or destructive, or right or wrong faltered. This equivocation increased the risk of escalation and confrontation. The balance was quivering with freedom and democracy under attack. This would move out of human control in the much-diminished new world order.

Chaos was opportunity. In the three years from 2020 the one per cent had pocketed twenty-eight trillion dollars of new wealth which was twice as much as the remaining ninety-nine per cent of the world's population.

Nation states were facing bankruptcy, allied to the rapid erosion of their authority. The age of individual economic sovereignty was really taking root and self-determining artificial intelligence was rapidly being applied to drones, pilotless aircraft and other armaments. Cyber money was testing the established norms of fiat money issued by governments.

This new economic culture; increasingly corrosive social division and belief systems; the steady decline of government influence; the stranglehold of technology; the increasing divide between democracies and autocracies; climate shift, taken together with the worldwide pandemic in the early part of the century, were the harbingers of greater more profound problems ahead. What followed was not anticipated and brought both despair and wonder.

The old world, consumed with consuming and seeking comfort in denial, had gradually realised the severity of rising temperatures but, as always, and despite desperate efforts, our differences overcame any shared views about what needed to be done. Agreement on a world wide scale proved elusive. No cohesive strategy could be agreed on.

Some made temporary, often token, strides to counter the inevitable decline sometimes at considerable economic cost to their populations. But climate change was relentless in the face of the absence of the necessary global actions urgently required to counter it.

Countries and their governments turned inward. Many pushed any action required into the distant future. It was all too much and populations were preoccupied with getting a better consumer life where success had been defined by carefully crafted lifestyle advertising.

Technology had facilitated the entrapment of both mind and body. And it certainly was not in the collective interests of the technocrats, or indeed their shareholders, to expedite ever-growing anxiety about the coming storm. Panic didn't sell.

So it was. Technology was the readily available and ever sophisticated channel through which populations, their aspirations, their likes and dislikes, their friends and enemies, their political affiliations, their very futures could be moulded, filtered, refined and eventually be determined. Cyber threat was increasingly used as a weapon as the world grew ever reliant on technology. A pernicious new silent and malign front to attack and reduce each other.

The dream of total control was within reach. Artificial intelligence was waiting in the wings to complete the picture as a willing accomplice. The relentless consumer machine linked to ever more sophisticated product placement saw to it that the old world remained detached from the massive catastrophe on its shoulder. Self-determination progressively eroded at the altar of duplicitous control and command.

Meanwhile, quantum computers were increasing their capacity to resolve the coming climate changes. By 2024, using multiple qubits, the number of entangled states on one processor was greater than the number of atoms in the then known universe. A truly staggering capacity which had the feeling of other worldliness. Another harbinger.

Chapter 2
Evolution Turns

By the mid-2020s heatwaves were already deadly for the more vulnerable, they overcame the body's ability to cool itself. Many weather stations at that time, across the world, had already recorded heatwaves surpassing this critical threshold. This survivability threshold was tested across the planet.

In 2022 around sixty thousand people died due to intense heat that summer. Nowhere was, as yet, unliveable but it was anticipated then that many regions would soon suffer, without respite, from bouts of intense heat and humidity.

The majority continued to be preoccupied with their own narrow lives. How easy it was for any latent curiosity they might harbour towards the oncoming crisis to be deflected by the technically created omnipresent drive to buy stuff and to value your life, and others, by how much stuff you or they had.

Sadly, even on the very edge of Armageddon, the sheeples headed for the cliff edge oblivious to their wider, fatal, end. We became, increasingly, detached from the light.

Global temperatures steadily increased, 2024 saw the hottest global month ever observed at

1.8 degrees above pre-industrial levels. Sea level increases were projected to prove critical for some one billion people by 2050. It was estimated that three billion would be living in places as hot as the Sahara desert by 2070.

The world population was set to reach eleven billion by the end of the twenty-first century. Twenty million people a year were being pushed out of their homes by climate fuelled disasters. But much worse was to come.

By the late 2020s the tipping points had already been reached. Intensified surface zones made it periodically dangerous to go out in some parts of the planet. The great melting of the Arctic and Antarctic sea ice was well under way. Oceans heated quickly and massive cyclones struck.

The chief carbon dioxide consumers, the forests, were logged incessantly and increasingly consumed by wildfires. Oceans were more acidic and hostile to marine life. Much of the world's population had by now migrated to urban areas – five billion lived in cities compared with one billion in 1960. The old world was still in denial.

But the narrow band of climatic fluctuations that the human race had enjoyed for some twelve thousand years was about to come to an abrupt end. These unusually stable climatic conditions had allowed the human population to surge from some five million people to more than seven billion in around ten thousand years.

Faced with global temperatures rising much quicker than forecast, the world was plunged into a global economic, social and environmental meltdown far quicker than even the most pessimistic projections.

Neither catastrophic flooding nor worsening migration in the 2030s realised unified action. New York and Miami had drowned, Los Angeles had no more water and together with San Francisco had been reduced to cinders by wildfires.

Not even catastrophic deaths in Europe, where there was minimal air conditioning, primed sufficient coordinated action. Sadly, by the 2040s, global temperatures were entrenched beyond human intervention and redemption.

The relentless antipathy between democratically elected governments and autocratic regimes did not help, as they played out a deadly game of interspersed global conflict, deploying more and more deadly autonomous weapons to devastating effect. In the midst of this desperate futile warfare, the more aggressive and profound climate change decimated equatorial lands and many cities were rendered uninhabitable.

At first thousands and then millions were on the move, dead or dying. The damage to the ecosystem was unimaginable. This massive progressive and unstoppable flood of the desperate and displaced was of biblical proportions, moving relentlessly like a plague of locusts determined to find somewhere on the planet where they would be safe.

A World Council was eventually formed in 2045. Alas, all too late. By now the climate change and migration levels were unmanageable and ungovernable. Any residual belief in institutions had disintegrated. Without structure, control and direction, social order collapsed piece by piece and day-by-day. Chaos was ready to fill the vacuum. Governments of all shades resisted, putting down ruthlessly rioting and social disorder. But to no avail.

Ruling factions around the world lost out to populations hell-bent on survival at all costs. Despite this, many countries managed to prioritise and put their emergency planning measures in play. Nuclear bunkers, long since turned into museums, had been restored, fully equipped for the disastrous and uncontrollable future. Lists of those in control and destined for those bunkers were drawn up.

The one per cent had seen to it that they had their fair share of private strongholds. Some few had left the planet. Nuclear reactors had been made as secure as possible and missile systems had long been rendered permanently inoperable, along with servers and computing systems, now burnt metal in seas of ash. Nobody remained to operate them and satellite and mapping services, together with phone and other computer-dependent systems, were now defunct.

For those few who still survived, many could not adapt to the withdrawal of their dependency drug, losing what life meant to them and no longer able to live their days endlessly scrolling virtual worlds where they felt safe and far removed from reality. Well, reality was now here at their door thrashing and heaving like a starving monster resentful at having been ignored for years.

Massive armaments stores around the world had been secured and abandoned. There had been a reluctance by some to decommission lest they be needed in the future. Such was the human drive to survive. Especial care had fortunately been afforded worldwide to the absolute permanent storage underground of potentially devastating biological weapons and the synthetic mirror images of molecules and bacteria. Yet another deadly arena which mankind should never have entered.

By the late 2040s currency had little or no value. The new world was no longer shaped by money or technology. However, as in ancient times and as in the two world wars in the twentieth century, gold had been garnered and hidden. Governments had secured their bullion in caves and mountains along with the treasures of their nations. And there they rested in perpetuity.

For the very few who had managed to outpace the incineration by fleeing towards the planetary poles, and for those already living in these climes, there was the prospect of temporary survival. For them, it was now all about what skills and experience you had to enable survival. In particular, how to grow and harvest foodstuffs and how best to garner and store water. Medical staff were in demand, as were fighters. No longer were you a slave to technology and its seduction.

A new social order took control. To survive you needed to defend what you had or take what you wanted. Guns were much sought after and fought for. Any type of armament demanded the same premium as food in this savage, brutal, barter economy. Steadily, the strong and armed took and they survived.

What very little of North America that had survived was a unique powder keg not only now home to the world's greatest gold bullion reserves but also many firearms. Worldwide, and by the mid-2050s, for the very few who had survived by moving north, violence and tribalism ruled.

Food was scarce. Production had halted. Medical care had ceased. Any remaining medical supplies and vaccines were, like nearly everything else, stockpiled for barter. In despair, many reverted to religion.

Nature marched on without remorse and with a complete disregard for human and animal decimation. Pests and disease thrived. Societal disintegration, like the relentless heating of the planet, closed like the hangman's noose. Brutal, without compassion and deadly.

Speculation was rife as to how much longer it would be before the tiny piece of the planet, which was still habitable, would be consumed. Many prayed for a saviour who might lead the world out of this crisis. There were a host of ethical and philosophical issues, such as how far should you go to protect those you love.

The dream of technological control by the few was a distant vision. This was Armageddon. Religion had foreseen a place where the kings of the earth, under demonic leadership, had waged war on the forces of good at the end of history. How right they were.

By 2060, those very few who still survived were desperate for salvation. Driven by starvation and a scorched planet, riven from all they knew and sought comfort from. Communication was back to medieval times, connectivity and mobility were distant memories. Almost all of the planet was a seething miasma of heat and completely uninhabitable. Not one screen shone anywhere.

As in centuries past, all was localised with surviving groups aligning for their survival and defence. There was no way of comprehending how any other survivors were coping with the disaster. People were suspicious and progressively inclined to the supernatural. They could no longer linger in a virtual world.

There had to be an answer to what had befallen the sophisticated human race. It was just incomprehensible. The few religious leaders who remained competed for power and control, very much aware that it would take a tremendous event to disseminate a unifying belief throughout any remaining populations and for that to gain some traction.

There was a great feeling of remorse and guilt. Scientists had foretold a tipping point which could be sudden and dramatic. Why did nobody really listen? What could have been done differently? Who was to blame? Such an utter waste. A civilisation gone in the blink of an eye. All that endeavour and achievement. Was this fate? Destiny?

And time was not on anyone's side. Those who trusted without question, and who were used and discarded, were again ready to follow. For salvation, for survival, for gain, for principle, who knew. People always looked to leadership when times were hard.

Chapter 3
Dark

She was born in 2061 into a family of four. Her name was Penumbra. Her community was on the west coast of Caledonia and her settlement was established in a glen at the heart of the ancient lands of Dalriada. Temperatures were extremely high and climbing. Barely liveable. The wall of heat was still moving inexorably north wreaking havoc, destruction and leaving total annihilation in its wake.

The roads and motorways could not be used, even by pedestrians, as the tar was constantly liquid with the temperature levels now prevailing. But headway was possible along the verges, except where many bridges had been swept away. Breathing was very uncomfortable, with no reprieve, day or night. Your chest often felt tight. Nights were the worst when thoughts roamed and anxieties festered.

She was a healthy robust baby but she had one unique characteristic. She possessed bright violet eyes. This went unnoticed at first. The slight Shadow that accompanied her was even less discernible. Penumbra well understood the Shadow.

Shadows are a guest, dependent upon the shining sun, a

passing memento to become nothing at all under a starlit sky. So, though shadows come as if part of a natural clock, in truth they tell more of golden rays than darkness. A shadow is an inanimate thing, meaning that it is not normally alive.

But the Shadow accompanying Penumbra was not a personification. Her Shadow was neither alive or dead or indeed any binary state between. It was evil in extremis. Vile, base and self-serving. Absent of a morally good will. Bent on wickedness.

The new world was vulnerable as was everything in it. As throughout old world history, human nature is about maximising individual payoffs at the expense of others including, at times, family members. When looking to the stars, many subscribed to an entity having created and now controlling our destiny. Others perceived the universe as having no design, no purpose, no evil and no good. Nothing but blind, pitiless indifference.

Her parents, Calum and Maihri, were well aware that her odd characteristics might draw unwanted attention, especially in their claustrophobic community. And they protected her. Penumbra was a rapid learner; disturbingly so. Knowledge was scarce. Strangely, she had seemingly limitless and effortless access to information at a time when information was at an all-time premium.

We had become so reliant on accessing our information from our screens which were now defunct. Some few libraries and bookshops survived but had been looted along with most other establishments. The level of civil unrest and criminal behaviour that had taken place, as the heat took hold and panic reigned, was way beyond what our planet had ever seen.

Her mother asked, "Tell me, our dear daughter, how at just five years old it is so that you act, speak and learn like a very clever twenty-year-old?"

"My mother, you know me but know me not. I love you but I am special, very special."

This was said in a disturbingly cold way, devoid of emotion and with more than a hint of malevolence. By seven years old her prodigious talent had become more evident to all. In the seventeenth century, she may well have been suspected of witchcraft.

The clan were unsettled and sought reassurance.

"What nature of child have you born? Is she from the dark world who has brought this apocalypse down upon us? We demand a trial," proclaimed a youthful camp follower. Calum could see trouble ahead and addressed the clan that evening. He was a proud man and fiercely protective of his daughter.

"My clan members, I am you and you are me. Together in this troubled new world. Much is unexpected and different. As is the ability of Penumbra. We need not fear this or her. We need abilities such as she shows to tackle the chaos before us and come out alive and living. Chaos breeds and welcomes opportunity. I understand your doubts. I share them. But there is much to do. Let us not turn on one another."

There were those that held their, still festering, suspicions of Penumbra. Her parents remained vigilant and frightened, ever aware of the danger to them and their beloved daughter. Over the following years their tight community thrived. Any doubts about Penumbra passed gradually with time as she continued to make a most useful and practical contribution in times that were very basic, threatening and brutal.

The lochs, lochans and rivers supplied an abundance of fish. And berries were still easily collected. But the unyielding hot and humid conditions led to widespread crop failures, often proved fatal to livestock and severely harmed aquaculture. Floods, droughts, storms and fires were regular life events, as were swarms of biting insects.

Penumbra knew full well that she was unique and had a purpose. Much of her time was spent observing her clan's engagement with the massive upheaval before them. She was a close observer of human behaviour. She noted, for example, that many still had their mechanical watches and how this enabled a record of time.

There was also a limited supply of batteries, not least for torches. Survival was the key and to do that you needed to defend what you had and take what you needed. As with her aptitude for rapid learning, so she took to acquiring formidable warrior skills. The clan had a champion and the day came when there was a competition for the honour to lead into battle.

Fighting in head to head combat in severe heat was exhausting and nights were just as harrowing as day. A rough piece of heather moor had been set aside just at the margins of the camp. Their shaman, Slame, conducted the procedure incanting, "We move to the beat of the dark one to save us all."

He drew a small circle with his totem stick forged from the antlers of a massive stag he had hunted and felled. The current champion, Magul, was a small but sturdy warrior, who moved like quicksilver.

His weapon was a small dirk in each hand which he handled with amazing dexterity and deadly skill. These were sgian dubh, an ancient Scottish knife concealed originally under the armpit. The larger butchering knife and the smaller skinning blade, both had antler handles. Opponent after opponent was dragged out of the circle either dying or dead, unable to challenge Magul's relentless carnage. All challengers beaten.

Penumbra raised her hand to match Magul saying to her parents and to her clan, "You were the ones who raised me and taught me. Believe me, I will become a heroic force to serve you, and all that is like you. You need not fear me. Because I will save you. Come forth Magul to meet your end."

"I Magul do not deal with children not yet to adulthood and women cannot take part."

Penumbra caught the eye of Slame, "If Magul fears a child woman then he is no champion."

Magul was enraged and motioned Penumbra to the circle. And so began the dance of death. No quarter was given. Her weapon was a long shafted dirk with a blade of strange dark metal, unknown to others and of a mysterious shade. With lightning speed, Magul struck again and again with both hands a blur.

Penumbra moved effortlessly very careful to fight within her human limitations. The everpresent, but discrete, Shadow accompanying Penumbra flickered in anticipation. She prolonged the exchanges, tiring Magul, minute by minute. As he slowed and his reactions diminished, she resolved to strike. Not to kill but sufficient to grind him to submission and leave him some honour. She struck easily, wounding him quite badly and he fell.

Penumbra faced away towards the dumbstruck onlookers. Magul rose like a snake and struck for her back. Pulling on her special powers, she pivoted like a hurricane and eviscerated him. Magul had fought dishonourably and the clan cheered her bravery.

Slame went into the circle, drew a chalk star on her forehead saying, "She moves like a mountain hare, strikes like an adder and brings survival to our clan. She is a good omen for us and a worthy champion."

Some two years later, in the year 2074, and without warning, one older member of the group came down with a fever and was stricken dead in a couple of days. Then a young male called Angus took ill.

Penumbra knew him and, unnoticed, went into his hut and touched his hand incanting, "By the Shadow, I rid you of your ailment."

By the next day news spread that he had had a miraculous recovery. Penumbra knew deep down what she could do and what her mission was. Of course, nobody else did. Nevertheless, she resolved then and there to exercise caution and to continue to refine her growing powers unnoticed.

On her sixteenth birthday, Penumbra, in 2077, was formally welcomed into the community as an adult. She cut a tall and imposing figure with a quiet authority that demanded respect. The Shadow around her emphasised the stark contrast between good and evil, innocence and corruption and truth and deception. Her eyes were magnetic and powerful. She was hardy, having survived steadily worsening conditions. The group had also had to withstand many raiding parties.

All had fighting skills and had experienced hand-to-hand combat. She excelled though and, following her victory to become their champion, was now the clan's prized warrior. Her brother Neil was also a formidable fighter and protector of his younger sister.

Penumbra sensed far stronger powers available to her at will but resisted. Slame was troubled by her abilities but was content to bask in her rise to the top of the clan hierarchy.

Penumbra took this opportunity to say to the gathered clan members, "The greatest danger in times of severe turbulence is not the turbulence itself but to act the way we did in the old world. New ways of doing and new ways of thinking are now needed to survive and thrive. The story of mankind begins with the first step and it is a new first step that we now need to take together, united and committed. Let darkness envelop you all."

The day came six months later. Wolf packs roamed wild, feral and unforgiving. Penumbra and Neil, together with their shaman, were on an exploratory forage some distance from their settlement roaming the glens and mountains. They had settled in for the evening by the loch side exhausted by the heat of the day.

Penumbra reflected on their day, "This wonderful country is so blighted by the heat. I swear the full beauty will be restored so that we might walk these bens and glens spreading the dark to settle into the very souls of the population."

Night fell, sullen and humid. Penumbra dozed ever wary in this wild land. With searing power, they attacked.

Penumbra yelled a warning, "Beware. Defend."

The gigantic drooling lead wolf had, in seconds, its slavering maw and putrid fangs just a split second away from her face. With lightning speed and force, Penumbra struck upwards slicing the wolf's throat with her long shank dirk, severing nearly completely the head of this proud massive wolf, hell-bent on destruction.

Neil cried out, "They overwhelm me sister. Bring forth the power I know you possess."

To her side, both Neil and the Shaman had defended bravely but under relentless attack from all quarters were now the worse for wear by the pack enraged at the loss of their leader. Neil could not get to his beloved yew bow and was about to die with four wolves ravenously stood over him. He had been badly bitten. She could see protruding bone. Penumbra lost control and, instinctively, released a surge of power that obliterated the pack. The Shaman stood transfixed.

Penumbra exhaled, "This is just the beginning priest. I shall bring forth such turmoil that this little planet never dreamed of."

Fleetingly, Penumbra was enveloped in a shroud of darkness and she possessed an air of cold calculating malice. The shaman moved to respond but turned away not daring to engage with her. Once more his ambition steered him to go along with Penumbra and hopefully benefit in the long run. Penumbra did not trust him and knew he would eventually turn against her.

Chapter 4
Light

In 2079 I lived in the centre of what had been the great cultural city of Edinburgh. I was twenty years old then. The historic skyline, with its magnificent castle on a volcanic plug was undiminished, albeit that everything in the city was being completely overwhelmed by the predatory heatwaves, scorching even the stonework. Care had to be taken if out too long.

Although moving indoors gave little, if any, relief. Anyone with breathing difficulties was in trouble or had died. It was a very challenging environment for the old and infirm. The predatory, ever present, heat took a heavy toll with the strongest and fittest the survivors.

In the absence of electrical power, one could not keep any food you might have. And it meant no facility to provide cold drinks which everyone was desperate for, faced with unrelenting heat and dehydration. Far too many of the population were lapsing into delirium, then unconsciousness before death took them. Old wells were opened up for cold fresh water supplies.

By then, there were rumours of a special figure in the west. Instinctively, I sensed wrongdoing and resolved to counter what I perceived as a harbinger of evil. I had, for some time, been concerned about the likelihood of evil grabbing the opportunities presented by the tumultuous cataclysm some of us had survived. And I just knew that this woman, although young, was trouble.

Power was very much in the hands of those who took it, regardless of the harm to others. It was reported to me that she demanded absolute allegiance and that her followers were ruthless. They claimed ownership of the new world and were said to worship the dark.

Specifically, it was claimed by travellers that this mythical figure had brought about singlehandedly the onset of a climatic reversal. A miraculous feat if true. Strangely, it seemed that temperatures, for whatever reason, had started very gradually to reduce, albeit it would take millennia to get back to temperatures at the outset of the twenty-first century. This possible reversal was being ascribed by some directly to this marvellous special leader.

Some called her the Star Bringer who, they claimed, was all seeing and powerful and who may have her origins from the mysterious universe and the stars. Her mission, allegedly, to save mankind from their folly. In troubled times any reprieve from disaster was heralded as fantastical and the Star Bringer had the halo of a miracle maker.

Many aspired to follow and to submit absolutely to what they hoped was a star prophecy that would bring all their troubles to an end and restore all that had been lost. There was certainly a craving for an answer to our troubles. Fertile ground for the supernatural to take root and flourish. And it did. Prophecies were already a feature of cultures with belief systems often attributing preternatural knowledge.

I was in hiding then, with a band of brothers and sisters who shared my beliefs. They were housed in Edinburgh castle's barracks, built in the late 1790s during the Napoleonic wars with France. Many, including the soldiers barracked there, had sworn fealty to me and to the cause – the eventual downfall of any star cult and all the evil intent they stood for. We had at that early stage, an encouraging thousand troops.

Well trained and equipped, from all walks of life. Male and female and a host of camp followers so necessary to support an army. Amongst them husbands, wives and their children. Some thirty or so with pistols and rifles. There was also an adequate supply of ammunition. But it would only last so long as new supplies were at an absolute premium.

We were very fortunate in the castle, having a steady supply of clean, cold and fresh water. The Fore Well in the castle first appeared in historic records in 1314 and had provided a vital lifeline to the castle's residents throughout many sieges.

All populations to the south had been, by now, decimated. No survivors. Those few clinging on at the edge of the death wall were resolved not to end up in a civilisation where superstition and primitive behaviour reigned. They believed that how our people had lived and loved had to be maintained whatever the cost. What remained was in real peril and civilisation could not fall to the dark ones.

Not all followers fully subscribed to the so called good life we had enjoyed.

"Max, you call us to the cause. But we really need to be clear just what that means my friend. The life we had has gone. Yes, we had what some would call the good life where there was the rule of law and a civilisation with urban areas, a surplus of food, a writing system and a division of labour. Then we had happiness, goodness and kindliness. But we also had terror, mutually assured destruction and many other ills and profoundly bad and corrupt wrongdoings. All was not well Max. We need to be very clear on our priorities," postulated Dramer.

Dramer was an interesting man, given to hyperbole and very gratified with the sound of his own voice. That said, he often got to the point that others had thought about but not expressed. He came from the old aristocracy, having had an extensive and rather grand estate in Northumberland passed down to him through the centuries. And was very lucky to have run north before the wall of heat.

His formal title was the Duke of Gramour. His stature and presence emanated breeding. Casual tweed clothing, slightly dishevelled, brown brogues, red socks, cap at jaunty angle and piercing blue eyes which spoke perpetual amusement.

He was more than happy to be called the Duke. As long as he realised he was just like everyone else now.

"Well Duke, you make some good points as always. Maybe we will get someone who will point the new way for us just as the dark side have. Who, other than us, can set the agenda for what is good. Let us start by asking our followers what it is we want. Easy to say, but we just want to survive this disaster," I replied as I swatted another blood sucking mosquito from the back of my neck.

My right hand warrior was Blocker, a mountain of a man hell bent on confronting the star movement. All accepted this would be a monumental task with the sheer energy and momentum gathering behind this evolving star campaign. Amongst planetary survivors, there was a seemingly unquenchable thirst for leadership no matter how brutal and unforgiving.

Disturbingly, the sheer ferocity of the cult was especially appealing to many. Absoluteness had always been corrosive, demanding from its believers total and absolute allegiance. On the other hand, there was the infinite strength in those committed to fairness, democracy and goodness. But they too could be uncompromising and intolerant of those not adhering to their doctrine.

The cult, led by Penumbra, continued to thrive in Dalriada set amongst the extremely hot northwestern climes of New Caledonia. We had to find a way to turn the populist tide and it's venal appeal. Very few wandered into our imposing stronghold.

Sadly, none from the south, now a lifeless cinder. Many headed northwest in search for the Star Bringer and so called miracle maker ensconced in the magical lands of Dalriada. Our camp was settled, with sufficient supplies and there had been much chat about how we were going to confront and bring down this star cult.

One day a young woman arrived. She was certainly different. I can't really say why. She stayed and, gradually, we got to know her. She gave little away. But there was a very noticeable personal characteristic – her eyes were a deep violet in colour and arresting. Her name was Aether. She said she was twenty-one years old. I wondered about that as she seemed to look different depending on who she was speaking to and what she was engaged in doing.

And an almost indiscernible Shadow followed her obediently. She spoke with fetching authority and her choice of clothing spoke control and suffused power. Black leather throughout. At her neck, a splendid gold torc resembling the coils of a snake. Somewhat reluctantly at first, I sought her advice and then, on an increasingly regular basis.

Aether mixed well with the troops and was often seen in conversation with Duke. They had a natural affinity. Their respective power and confidence bouncing off each other. Both knew the road ahead would be tough and bloody but displayed a reassuring belief in

our cause and that goodne·
would prevail in this new world.

The Duke often reflected on just what that meant, "Aether, as you know, much has been said and written about goodness. Certainly not the same for everyone. When crafting our strategy to take on the dark, I suggest we keep it simple and don't get into complex interpretations and philosophical perambulations. There would be no end to it. Good and bad are basic and clearly defined in people's minds."

When I felt I had Aether's trust, I set out in detail our objectives and the extent of the challenge ahead.

Inclining her head of blonde braided hair, "My dear Max, I am put here to aid your campaign and counter those who would cast an evil net on your precious planet, 'heir disciples supplicant

ഗ

nd nefarious ends. This

...ot stand. And you can look to me to support you in this quest."

She was, undoubtedly, very special. And I had, for some time, dwelt over just what she was. Was she alien. What was her special mission.

Steadily, our campaign grew recruiting more and more souls to our campaign. There was, of course, much suspicion in the camp with fears that the star cult now had sufficient time and ability to infiltrate our ranks.

"We do not have the strength and depth to match this magical Star Bringer. How can we hope to match such black magic. They will slaughter us all and yet who, other than us, can resist such horrors?"

commented a respected camp lieutenant.

One forbidding moonlit night all slept in the castle barracks. Any potential assassin that had plans to kill would first have to scale precipitous cliffs and, having achieved that difficult feat, overcome hard bitten fully trained guards. Unseen and undetected, a black shadow scaled the northern cliff of the castle. The interloper did so in complete silence and with disturbing ease.

On reaching the ramparts, this ghostly presence alighted beside a guard and ran his obsidian blade ruthlessly across the guards throat severing his windpipe. Then, he gently lowered the unfortunate soldier to the ground. The barrack door stood unlocked.

The Star assassin entered, their black blade venomous and glinting in the moonlight. The room was large and bleak with a high coffered ceiling. It was completely dark and suffocatingly stagnant. The reek from hundreds of unwashed, prostrate, skanking sleeping bodies was gagging. The darkness engulfed the dark.

It was the most piercing darkness ever – it was not merely the darkness that came out of the absence of light, it was much more sinister. The interloper brought this with him like a shroud and, having eventually found me, was just aligned to strike.

From nowhere, the light of Aether alighted like a sword, severing with one blow the interloper's dagger hand. The howling assassin, with a star struck into his forehead, turned, smiled and struck again with his other arm wailing, "the masters shall smite those against us and dark energy prevails."

Many awoke suddenly from their fitful slumbers as, before their eyes, the malign intruder was then completely and utterly eliminated. No vestige remained. My mind was in hyperdrive and severe shock. What we were up against was put into clear and stark focus. But oh, the ferocity of Aether. This was something else. I thought then about the forces we mere humans would encounter on our quest.

I then turned to Aether and the army, now all fully focused on the scene before them. Candles were lit.

Much chatter and awe as I addressed them "Friends, the dark

forces got to me here. The killer's blade at my very throat. Who saved me? Our Aether that's who. Yes, she does possess special powers. Powers that we need to survive the dark unknown forces at our very door as we sleep. Together with Aether, we can prevail. Let us do just that. Few remain on this beloved planet and it falls to us, the good few, to plough a sacred road to our brave new world."

Aether looked out of the small castle window seemingly looking through and beyond the dark layer of cloud floating just beneath the high up castle ramparts.

"Now it begins and it shall be brutal my friends. We face determined opponents who will bring forth all from the dark side. Fear not. I am strong, deadly and have much more to offer you as our campaign moves remorselessly forward," she incanted.

That night the battlements were in turmoil, consumed with preventing more assassins striking. Those already traumatised, and running scared, added fuel to the fire with their leader proclaiming, "We knew this would happen. They are amongst us. Look to your families. Our cause is just. But we need to talk about what we do from here."

Later the next day I decided to speak to Aether. The conversation was difficult. She was calm, controlled, almost spiritual and looked me appraisingly in the eye.

"I heard the intruder and acted quickly to counter the attack. I had to bring forth some unusual powers handed down to me. And would ask you Max to please say nothing of this as it could work against us and our cause."

"No Aether, we cannot postpone any longer. Many in the camp are doubtful about taking our campaign any further. Their leader, Tradger, is resolute and determined to question our direction of travel. I think he has considerable support from our clan members. You really need now to say more about what you are and what you can do for them. They need convincing."

"I hear you Max. I will address the clan. Please make the necessary arrangements."

Before doubts solidified to rebellion, I set the scene for a clan gathering that night. Braziers were set on the castle battlements. Aether stood proud; her striking silhouette emblazoned starkly against the firelight cast over the castle. The night was hot and pallid, redolent of something strange and unexpected.

Expectations were high, word having spread beyond those present in the barracks about the fate of the assassin. There were many who speculated. Not a few were alleging dark arts at work. Aether knew persuasion was required. She remained still. The crowd silenced. Still she stood.

Then, slowly at first and raising her right hand pointing skywards, a brilliant blast of sheer energy burst forth increasing steadily until all fell on their knees blinded by the ferocity of the light force. Then, when all before her were supplicant and subdued, she gently said, "Fear not my friends. You know me. But there is more. I come to you with powers you have never seen or dreamt of. I have a clear mission. The same mission as you. But you need something magical to counter the Star Bringer. And I have that magic. Magic is dangerous. It is neither good nor bad, right nor wrong. My friends, it can either be a blessing or a curse. It takes the strength of the magic wielder to make the magic their own. To make it serve that person and not the other way round. I am in complete control of my powers."

Loud gasps rang forth from the multitude. Some ran away. But most were wrapped in her charms. Embraced by her powers. Submitted to her authority. Filled with new hope. Empowered by her might and magic. Enthralled by her presence. She would lead them. She could do it.

Aether drew back her energy from the stars and night descended once more with a light wind sending flickering shadows on to the castle walls. She stood tall and mighty. Completely unafraid and supreme.

"You have witnessed tonight a mere fraction of the powers I possess and can put at your disposal. I know there are those who fear our enemies and we should not underestimate them. But you are not alone. I stand with you to the end and their eventual annihilation. We will, together, smite these predators and cleanse them, and their dark corruption, from this our beloved planet. Join with me and Max in our mission. Bring in the light."

As one, the followers rose in adulation of their saviour, yelling out her name again and again.

They would follow. And Aether knew it. More and more, Aether proffered advice on strategy and planning. She was at my side most of the time. In fact, I sensed she rather liked me and, in turn, I was a little surprised at the feelings I had for her. Aether was well aware of just what she was capable of and what her mission was but the full extent of this was just for her to know at this stage.

Penumbra was formidable and all would have to go right to wrest power from her and the Star Masters. Much was at stake and Aether had a clear vision. She was not without her own view as to what humans were for.

Whilst relieved at such a figure coming in support of the cause, I still had reservations and was concerned that this situation could get out of control. I did, however, find her oddly attractive and I could not stop myself from looking at her. And I suspected Duke felt the same.

Aether was an immortal and could shift into whatever presence was necessary for her mission. She was fully cognisant of the reproductive process undertaken by the human species, the attendant sexual proclivities involved and the incomprehensible concept of love.

She was absent of emotion and feelings. Within the claustrophobic confines of a seething massed community, she had often heard and sometimes accidentally witnessed, this species fulfilling their purpose like the animals they were.

Nevertheless, Aether was skilled in the assessment of beings.

The Duke of Gramour did possess a certain insouciance and bearing borne of centuries of privilege and in breeding. However, she sensed the Duke would become an obstacle and his strategic role would have to be progressively eroded. Max was a different matter: for some reason she could not tie down, she saw something hopeful in him.

Chapter 5
Star Cult

Her brother and the Shaman were awestruck at the annihilation of the wolf pack by Penumbra. She knew this was a pivotal moment and that she had to seize the initiative. A star shape suddenly became emblazoned across her brow as if by magic and it would continue to shine there brightly. Thus, was the great star cult initiated.

On their return to camp, Neil spoke strongly in her support, "Behold we have amongst us an anointed one to lead and protect us and smite our enemies. She bears the mark."

The Shaman, although jealous, sensed opportunity for himself. It was enough. The deposed leader of the clan – an arrogant evil man answering to the name Vargo – left camp the next day cursing and vowing vengeance.

"She may think she is special. Knife blades know no special. They maim and kill, magic or not. I will return. You may abase and degrade yourselves before her, a stranger who will, believe me, let you down and turn against you. She will render you submissive and neutered. Beware my friends. Save yourselves. Follow me."

Penumbra grasped the opening this presented, pulling her considerable forces together into a common cause. All followers over twelve years of age were branded with a star on their forehead. There was reluctance and some resistance, but insufficient to deflect Penumbra who held her followers in thrall and subservient.

The gospel of the star was preached. There was to be no compromise in this post-apocalyptic new world. New rules for a new order. Much would be made of how they had begun to pull back climate decline and how they would rule a new world order. Any detractors remaining met quick and final retribution.

Penumbra knew the next step she had to contrive. Her final destination was far to the north and she knew it would be an arduous and dangerous trek where she and her followers would be wide open to the foul do-gooders hell-bent on stopping her mission. That would not happen. The Star Masters would prevail and darkness would envelop all.

The now vast community was anyway having difficulty surviving where they were with insufficient food supply and shelter. Now was the time to set forth for the north. And Penumbra was very ready to lead towards her destination.

And so the trek began. The main roads were an obvious route to take whenever possible, albeit that you could not walk on the tacky tar. But often it was possible to walk alongside the roads, saving time and avoiding obstacles such as river valleys and other difficult topography. Rumours were brought into camp about a saviour like figure with a very different vision of a future of the new world. A vision far removed from that of her star cult. Penumbra knew instinctively who she faced. That would wait.

The future she was there to deliver would be delivered. The Star Masters had decreed it so. Her Shadow quivered with suppressed delight. Penumbra's followers were zealots, steeped in self-righteousness and totally given over to badness and the dark. There was no thought given as to what is good and what is bad. They were bad and it felt just right. No quarter would be given. The good would be gone, eradicated. The new world suitably cleansed.

They encountered many communities as they moved northeast through the highlands of

Caledonia and Penumbra saw to it that she inveigled them into the cause. There were difficulties. Several clan leaders, their strongly held territory threatened, resisted bravely and pushed to confrontation. Sometimes in face to face combat and there were also broader and prolonged fearsome exchanges. Such opposition was, for the most part, summarily dispatched without remorse or challenge.

The mother of all major battles took place quite soon after leaving their established stronghold. A fearsome brigand, who had recent military experience, had pulled together some former colleagues to establish a slick fighting force experienced in and equipped with high powered weaponry.

He went by the handle of Grinder. A small weasel like figure dressed in military fatigues and who had advance knowledge of Penumbra's march north. And was determined to grasp the opportunity that presented itself. Grinder even moved like a weasel, squat, low to the ground and with a touch of the feral about him.

It was the second night out from Dalriada in Appin. The massive army had eventually bedded in for the night. There were those still whiling away the evening at sporadic campfires.

One soldier, tired and hungry, blurted, "I fear a little to say but our leader, although impressive, has more than a touch of the dark about her. I have the faith. But doubts too," as he shivered, despite the hot humid night.

No sooner had he spoken, than the sound of rapid gunfire shattered the quiet. To his practiced military ear, it sounded like several hundred rounds a minute. He knew that his army had some guns but was immediately concerned. The rapid rhythmic staccato bursts continued unabated followed by screaming and wailing.

The camp was in turmoil. Exchanges of gunfire filled the air. Many were badly wounded and killed. In short shrift. The Grinder's entourage was an efficient killing machine. The weasel squealed. The battle ground on relentlessly.

Roaring in blind fury, the army gathered it's forces and the camp multitude hacked bravely into those dispensing a deadly wall of bullets. With sheer numbers, they gradually eroded the attackers. It was bloody, it was brutal, it was epic and it was heroic. Claymores and dirks brought death and mayhem. The warriors, with almost mesmerising speed, glided into the sheer keening momentum of the event becoming intoxicated with the exhilaration of battle.

The flash of blades rising and falling, the music of battle. They were fully committed to the defence of their cause and their loved ones. The cacophony of feet, the pounding of drums and the skirl of bagpipes drowned their kinsman's and kinswoman's songs of valour and groans of despair. Many died.

The protagonists eyes were whitened in abject terror as they rushed to their fates, followed by the shuddering fighter on fighter contact. The jarring impact and splinter as weapons pierced through shields and armour. As bullets eviscerated. Everywhere the enemies grappled and hacked.

Dirks skewered and ripped flesh and blood spurted skywards. The air sang with pain. Pipers played over this dance of death. Whatever the cause, it now came down to survive being maimed for life or brutally shredded to a pulp.

Then Penumbra strode forth wreathed in her Shadow, "Hear me warriors. War calls forth all that is honourable in us and our cause is just. We will prevail. And I am here amongst you. Behold."

The Shadow divested itself from its host and languidly stretched ether like towards the enemy. Hungrily, like some ancient monster, it devoured them one by one as they just disappeared. Suddenly all was silent. The din no longer. Weapons laid down. Any enemy soldiers remaining, surrendering.

There was absolute carnage. Debris, much human, scattered absently across the camp site. Then the grim task of tidying this ocean of confusion and sorrow. Like all armies, there were the soldiers' wives and children together with the human and other detritus following the campaign.

Penumbra addressed the camp the next morning, "We have lost many dear to us. I applaud your bravery. We must acquire more armaments and the skills to deploy them effectively. We will and we remain on course. Together we will vanquish those who would oppose us. Believe in the power of the dark. Now we continue the clearance and tonight we relax and enjoy."

Preparations for the evening festivities began. And although there was grieving, there was also a sense of excitement. Plans were made and relished by the survivors.

"We will dance and feast. Music and fun. A chance to remember those who have gone and make those who will replace them. Send forth our hunting parties and food gatherers," commanded Penumbra.

It was a wild night. All the pent up pressures released like the floods they faced daily. There were confrontations and couplings. All aided by the usual steady supply of Usquebaugh. Whisky stills travelled with the army and were essential to morale.

The drone of the pipes thrust a melancholy tone skywards mixing with the mood of many as the whisky spirit took control of their emotions. The hardest hearts surrendered to the haunting mellifluous sad language of the pibroch floating across the camp as dawn broke.

As well as major attacks, they encountered many personal challenges. One such was against a mighty beast of a warrior who excelled with the claymore. For his bulk he was agile and full of guile. Penumbra was always careful to stay, whenever possible, within the very limited confines of her considerable human skills. For the most part that would suffice. But this time he was a truly doughty opponent.

So, she lent gently on her powers, prolonging the exchange cutting methodically with her dirk until the giant fell exhausted with blood loss. Once recovered he became a leading warrior completely devoted and ruthless in advancement of the cause. His name – Reaper. A sadist.

Disease and hunger took many. There was a constant thrum of invisible biting insects, thirsty for letting blood. The silent feeders, mosquitoes, had come north with a vengeance. Their syphon like mouth parts pierced the skin and fed on our blood unnoticed. A system fine-tuned over millions of years. They spread disease – malaria, Nile virus, dengue and yellow fever.

Various unguents were developed and tested to halt this invasion. But few worked. Their biting and constant presence, both through daytime and through hot humid nights, hit morale hard. More and more whisky stills were made as an antidote. The medical unit were hard pressed.

In this new world, a doctor was king. The few surviving were hard pressed. Conditions were about as bad as they could be. Lack of basic equipment, even bandages and salves. The antibiotics and other medications needed were as rare as a cool day in this festering hell.

As with books, the massive looting had emptied pharmacy shelves very early on and, such supplies that remained, were bartered. So, medical staff did the best they could. And very many of the clan went to the stars earlier than they would have done in the now defunct old world.

Penumbra took command of all marriage and funereal activity using her magic to bond the living and incinerate the dead. And so, her power base was enhanced and the Star Bringer myth grew and spread far and wide. It was a powerful message in turbulent times.

But the temperatures continued to wrought havoc. Whilst not yet at the incinerating levels which had set most of the old world ablaze, the heat was severe.

Those trees and plants remaining were struggling. Rivers were flooding dangerously and regularly. Mountain streams were often in torrents. And the combination of the ferocious heat and heavy rainfall made the going very slow. Keeping clean and healthy was difficult.

The intense heatwaves from the south combined with clinging humidity, pests, infection, disease, cramped basic living conditions and the absence of care produced a very unhealthy cocktail that took many more early to the stars.

The army came up the shores of Loch Ness. Encampments were set each evening and the considerable task of shelter and provisioning put in train. Latrines had to be dug and tents set. The primary concern was food. This could be taken from nature, stolen by raiding parties or bought.

The last option sometimes involved finding local allies to supply food in exchange for military support. An element of chain supply was also achieved with forward moving soldiers engaging communities on the planned route.

Everyone lived in the clothes they stood in and they all stank. Personal hygiene was completely neglected by her disciples adding to the toll brought about by disease, famine and pestilence. Periodically, but not often enough, the opportunity presented itself to bathe in the lochs. And so, many that evening washed their clothes and bathed. Their disturbance of the calm waters did not go unnoticed.

That dark sultry night, whilst the exhausted slept, burnt out by the constant demands of a travelling life, the monster struck swiftly from the loch. It was enormous, heavily scaled and fast. Shelters were swept away and people fled in blind panic. Some turned to meet the creature, brandishing flaming torches. The beast doubled its attack, moving quickly through the camp shattering all before it. Many lay dead, wounded and dying.

It was as if the monster had a mission heading unfailingly

towards the Star Bringer. The thing reeked to high heaven. Much worse than the camp latrines on a very hot day. It's eyes were a hellish deep red filled with the promise of Armageddon.

In the midst of this turmoil, Slame strode out to meet the beast incanting, "Get ye back to your lair ye demon spawn before the Star Bringer smites you down."

There was mild amusement in those terrible eyes. With one languid sweep of the monster's tail, the shaman's startled head was parted from his quivering body. The monster sniffed and turned to meet its target – the evil Star Bringer.

Penumbra was on a knife edge fully realising who had set this beast loose. Calm, collected and confident she walked steadily to meet this monstrous adversary. Brute force was no match for her magic. Nevertheless, she would need to be cautious until she knew just what powers were available to this very ancient predator brought into action by the dramatic heating of the loch waters and under the direction and some degree of control by the Star Sisters.

The two colossal forces now faced each other with what remained of the camp looking on spellbound. The monster struck first inflicting a passing glance to Penumbra. The speed unsettled her and the slight touch of its tail on her right arm quickly began to spread to her body. Poison and quick acting. Penumbra found it difficult to pull on her powers.

A unique experience. Sensing her dilemma the beast struck

again, sweeping her legs away. The pain intensified and Penumbra became disorientated. At that critical moment, a warrior plunged his longsword deep into the back of this beast. It was just enough of a respite for the Star Bringer to release a deadly searing blast that rendered the monster motionless.

She then strode forward languidly, was passed a double headed war axe, looked the distressed beast in the eye and beat it's head to a pulp. When cleaved, an unctuous putrid green liquid poured down from it searing the ground and forming a deep cess pit. And oh, the stink. Silence fell in the encampment followed by ecstatic thumping of shields to acknowledge a magnificent vanquishing of a truly formidable enemy.

Penumbra raised her right hand in salutation, "Behold my star children. Look. Look, what we can achieve. The forces of those who oppose us are as nothing compared to my powers and other powers I may call on at will. Together we can set aside goodness and mercy. Your star will lead you. Embrace hate. I do."

The followers stood awestruck, the stars on their foreheads throbbing in unison. They were the star children to the end.

Penumbra had a clear idea of the destination. She was aiming for a small island just to the north of the much larger Caledonia where they would eventually set sail from. There she would establish her Star Court and there stood the ancient star gatherer site. But they had many miles of difficult rivers and mountains yet to travel.

And so, the campaign ploughed northeast following main roads for the most part. Many died. Insect life had embraced climate change and many lethal ones had been swept north. Fevers were common and especially bad in these flow lands. The biting was unrelenting and dispiriting.

Penumbra had to lead and led strongly from the front being ever present to help and support and do all she could to maintain morale. It became an ever demanding role as the trudge through these inhospitable domains took its toll.

The days, weeks and miles ground on, groups associating themselves with the cause and joining the trek. They brought news and disease and were not always welcome. These were treacherous times. You trusted nobody.

Suspicion was endemic. In their turn, any newcomers were assessing what they had aligned themselves to. In time, common cause was established. But there were always more to be fed and cared for. And the unpredictable waiting for the weak and unprepared.

In time, Penumbra's massed army reached the flow lands with its malicious network of bottomless pools interspersed amongst acre after acre of moss, floating like some giant sponge ready to suck, pull and entomb those who came within its grasp. Sticking to the roadside, their journey proved uncomfortable but uneventful. There was just one more day ahead in this hell hole and the camp was settling down for the night beside the bogland which ran right up to the road.

Gently at first there was a wobbling from below the mossy landscape. Almost like sitting on a boat. They were used to this. But imperceptibly the swell established a disturbing and threatening rhythm. Anxious eyes looked out. The first victims were sucked into dark deep pools broiling and erupting as a giant tentacle struck out. Many sickening tentacles followed. The beast was hungry and there was a plentiful supply above.

The Star Bringer was growing weary of the reach of the Star Sisters and beckoned forth more support and power from her Star Masters. It came instantly.

Levitating in a swirl above the ancient flow lands, she radiated sheer power and venom. The beast from below sensed danger and a calcified enormous red beak opened up from the pool in challenge. Her forehead seared a dark laser like shaft at her target.

The adjoining pool and the very ground beneath them shuddered and then, suddenly, all was quiet and settled as if nothing had happened. The clan spent a very unsettled night and had struck camp well before sunrise.

That next day they came out of the bogland and the insects relented slightly. Before them now were shallow limestone lochs rich with brown trout. A rare opportunity to refresh and relax.

Penumbra addressed her star children once more, "The Star

Sisters, along with their tiresome belief in goodness, have tried once again to thwart our endeavours. As before friends, they failed utterly. They are weak. They will fail. We will bring darkness to the few who remain on this planet."

The clan had available many skills and abilities. Amongst them were some excellent musicians. Dougie was the best. His fiddle playing almost sacred. A modest man with uncanny talent. Expectation was high that evening when all were settled round campfires with food in their bellies. They were ready to dance.

Dougie had nursed his ancient fiddle like a newborn. The humidity was not helping but whoever had crafted it had imbibed it with something magical and it held a note like no other. Dougie was made to play it and that he did. Sparingly, but what an event when his talent met the strings.

Dougie sat centre stage. Silence fell. The very land listened. No one spoke or as much as coughed. The first note was struck. Perfect pitch and perfect tone. What followed was a haunting tune that trapped your very soul. Rising in tempo pulling your inner self upwards to a unique place. A happy place of your own making.

Gradually his hand began to flow like liquid silver thumping out an irresistible beat. It pulsated. It drew you in. It trapped you. Nothing else mattered. The beat. Young and old rose and started to dance.

Oh, the joy. Dougie really got going. Sheer joy fled forth from his instrument. His hand now a blur together with the dancers before him. And so it continued well into the night. Dougie never faltered. This was what he lived for and what his fiddle was made for. The camp was late to start the next morning. But spirits had been revitalised and were unusually high.

Barren land followed them. Standing stones cast their shadow which was felt by all who passed by them. They had, in their ancient presence, some strange effect. You felt you were being looked at and assessed and found wanting. Fields were no longer withholding sheep, the borders not marked by stone dykes but by large vertical slabs of slate. A landscape of monoliths. A landscape of magic. Penumbra knew she was coming home.

Eventually, the still massive army reached the north coast of

Caledonia. A turbulent strait of sea stood between them and their destination. Boats were scarce. The crossing would be dangerous. Very dangerous. Plans had been set in advance but Penumbra knew that this was going to be a long haul.

In the event, given the number of followers, shipping them took many weeks across a frothing seething stretch of water where some of their meagre craft foundered, reducing still further their small fleet. But make it they did and in sufficient numbers. The island was New Orkney.

It had been a very fertile land and even now had a vestige of that richness remaining. So, it was there that the Star Court was established. Next to the ancient standing stones of The Ring Of Brodgar. And

Penumbra adopted, formally, the mantle of Star Bringer

"I now stand before you in this stygian gloom as the Star Bringer. From this ancient site I will call forth dark devastating powers against those who are set to oppose us and take over our world and the life we want. I will not fail you. You have already witnessed how I have turned back the deadly climate change. More will follow."

She was unassailable and completely dominant. They were her children : she was their shepherd.

Chapter 6
Stone of Destiny

And so began the next mass migration. Aether knew well the game she was specially selected to play. And that the future for our planet centred on a small island with ancient magical roots and where the stars could be called on. So, the plan was to depart from our stronghold at Edinburgh Castle, moving slowly north, heading eventually to the northern coastline of New Caledonia. Aether was aware of the value of enabling me to continue to lead. I had my doubts about our collective ability to counter this dark cult.

Aether advised, "If people are not scared they do not worship and if they do not worship they cannot be led. There are many roads to worship: love as well as hate."

As always, the Duke was ready with the riposte, "It may be wise Aether not to have our followers too much in your thrall. There is, as you know, a fairly thin line between being dedicated to a cause and besotted and supplicant to it."

By then, we were well aware of the exponential growth of the cult and their trek to the north. There would be a reckoning. But first there needed to be a distinctive recognition of our cause. Aether and I had long ruminated over this and the importance of countering the star symbol. Whatever was selected had to have real significance to our avid followers. The impetus our campaign had was very encouraging and it was crucial to maintain this.

There was a mythical beast adopted by the old Caledonia. It was the unicorn. Caledonia's national animal. In Celtic mythology the unicorn was a symbol of purity and innocence and there were many tales of dominance and chivalry attributable to the magical mysterious unicorn. Aether sensed the significance of such a symbol. And she had a plan.

Just what was needed to galvanise and sustain the long campaign we knew lay ahead. There would be doubts and defections which would need to be assuaged whilst taking our supporters with us and our campaign.

She addressed our clan army saying, "The road ahead will be hard and demanding. We will be met by strange forces. But we are here now to save our new world from those dark forces hell-bent on supreme power. To aid our cause, we will adopt an ancient Scottish beast – the mighty unicorn. A mystical symbol of what is right and honourable. We will, together, triumph against the dark side threatening to undermine our new world."

Her followers needed no prompting, taking the unicorn to their hearts and minds. Thus was the unicorn as a banner symbol born. Using her special powers, Aether saw to it that all our followers had a unicorn emblazoned on their right hands adding to it just a speck of starlight. As night settled over the campsite one could see the tiny suggestion of this special light emanating from each follower. Like a barrier against wrongdoing and darkness.

A key resting place on their long campaign to the north was the ancient city of Perth, once the capital of Scotland. It was where Scotland's Royal Court was held with their monarchs crowned there over hundreds of years. To reinforce the democratic base of their cause, a fully representative Unicorn Court was established by Aether and it, in turn, elected Aether as their Queen.

To formally mark the significance of the movement, and Aether's place in it, the ancient Stone of

Destiny was used at her coronation as it had been done for monarchs for centuries. The Unicorn Queen slid comfortably into her new regal mantle. Her mission was on target. The Star Sisters would be content. Ours was not a cult but a democratic movement. The Stone of Destiny went with us.

Revitalised, the army got under way striking out north again. Their path often took them round the mountainous scenery, along glens which followed ancient riverbed runs with deep cut steeply sided valleys and also more broadly based glaciated valleys.

One sultry afternoon we were plodding through yet another glen with a river running alongside and all looking forward to setting camp for the evening. Suddenly the air chilled, the chatter stopped, birdsong faltered and a wolf howled nearby.

Then an ominous inky black cloud swept down from the hillside. A massive murder of crows swooped low over the army, screeching, their wings flapping like shrouds in a straining breeze.

All this heralding a bent old woman dressed all in black from head to toe. At her side, pranced a mythical amarok, a giant wolf said to hunt alone rather than in a pack and feast on those foolish enough to hunt alone at night. As she shuffled down the sheep track lined by wilting bracken and gorse, all movement in the glen stuttered and ground to a halt.

There was no mistaking her presence. Short, with a long hooked nose and wherever she moved a black shimmer moved with her like a devoted servant. Unerringly, this darkness moved towards Aether, halting in front of her.

Aether was wary. This could be the power she could not contain. The old woman raised her head wearily. She had black holes where eyes normally shone. Yet she could clearly see.

This strange apparition spat out, "Aether, you should know that the Shadow will come." She then turned away cackling and faded to nothing. Aether knew full well the implications of this prophecy but had no intention of sharing this knowledge. Indeed, she would do all she could to prevent it coming to pass.

To reassure, Aether addressed her followers, "Another attempt by the dark to diminish our quest. This will not stand. We will prevail for the light."

The parade north was a weary one, but they too garnered many to their cause. The denizens were restless and anxious wondering which way this weird new world would go. Slowly there was a wider awareness settling that there now existed two quite distinct and opposing cultures heading for a clash which would determine much in a very uncertain future.

"People need to be afraid to fight. If they are not scared, they do not worship."

The army moved very slowly through the massive Grampian plateau littered with mountains and deeply glaciated glens but, once again, their passage was immensely aided by the road network. Food was the constant demand and the glens were full of hordes of biting insects and clan brigands.

But Aether knew more was needed to aid their cause. Her powers were massive and, as yet, untapped and untested. And so, she called for a Meet to address the massed supporters.

Standing above the crowd on a small heather clad knoll, she looked radiant dressed in white hide and armed to the teeth. Her eyes blazed. She knew this had to be a moment of historic significance that would resonate for millennia.

The Star Masters must be defeated to avoid the post climatic world descending to absolute dictatorship, with the population reduced to willing victims, totally controlled and manipulated at the whim of the Star Bringer and the

Star Masters. The adoring Blocker looked up in admiration and blind obedience. Aether reached out raising her right hand and from it emanated a ray of stunning light reaching out to a distant hill.

And there, suddenly fully formed, a living unicorn shining white and truly regal appeared. Aether looked on proudly as the crowd parted and the unicorn cantered towards her and, once at her side, never left it. Together they were majestic. Power emanated from them. This was a force to be reckoned with. Aether addressed her followers

"We are the force for good chosen to strike down the evil brought to us by the cult led by the Star Bringer. The greater good always comes at personal cost: always. And our just cause is the cost each of you bear. Goodness is all."

Her proud followers, now prostrate before her, raised their unicorn hands in adulation and salutation together and chanted, "You Aether, our Unicorn Queen, will smite the wicked and bring peace and order to our new world." They waved their right hands glowing in unison and salutation.

As usual, the Duke cautioned Aether against being too evangelical and dogmatic counselling, "You must take great care to orchestrate the full involvement of our followers in the process. Without them there would be no mission for the light."

Heading further north the revitalised campaign made good progress for a while. Any energy or enthusiasm was though easily diminished. Yet another glen with a river running through was selected for the night. It just looked the same as all the others. It was not. News of the army had by now spread. Beacons on mountain tops and ridges had been signalling this and others had an eye on securing diminishing food supplies and power.

Night fell. All that could be heard was the chatter of the river and the odd hoot from an owl, interspersed with the howl of wolves. There were many, they were well armed and they were fearless. The camp had rich pickings and survival was all. There would be no quarter. And, although outnumbered, surprise and guns were in their favour.

All hell broke loose as they forded the river to the camp. The defence was robust and fierce but bullets found their mark and hope slowly bled away. Many died or were wounded. Although precious supplies were kept safe. The Blocker was cutting swathes through the brigands with his claymore but he was no match for a bullet which took him in the leg.

Aether was incensed. She knew there would be trouble. Some natural in this troubled world. Some attributable to the Star Masters. This had to be met head on. She strode up to the leader, a bear of a woman. Arrows flew from both sides in every direction. Nothing touched Aether. There was a dull halo enveloping her. Her unicorn, as always, by her side.

Her opponent, a magnificent woman warrior at over six feet tall and carrying a repeating pistol, circled Aether. She had a patch over her left eye, closely cropped dark hair, with a long scar running like a red thread from her hair line to her chin and she was a killer.

She fired repeatedly at Aether without warning. Aether had dealt with technology much beyond the physics of ballistics. Indeed, beyond the dimensions and understanding of this primitive world. No bullet reached her. But, with a wistful flick of her hand, she shredded her opponent. Word spread quickly and the onslaught hesitated.

Aether projected her voice, "Raiders hear me, you can all be wiped away just with my voice. Do not resist. Instead, join with us, enjoy our food and pledge allegiance with a unicorn emblazoned on your right hand."

They were wary but their eyes did not deceive them. There was a wonderful unicorn standing proud before them. They ceded and joined the campaign. They would be watched carefully.

Word of the unicorn and the Unicorn Queen spread like wildfire in the Highlands. As the massed followers shuffled north more and more came to submit and serve. On reaching Inverness, her army waited patiently, recruiting steadily those coming in hope. Armaments were made and food supplies established with scouting parties sent out ahead. Guns were available but in very limited quantities. A number were taken. Some bartered.

Gradually I ceded the key leadership role to Aether, taking most supporters with the transition.

There were still though those who had doubts about Aether. Understandably so, given the weirdness surrounding her. The Duke was her cheerleader, taking every opportunity to sing her praises when speaking to her followers.

"Friends, Aether is magnificent. How fortunate are we that we have her amongst and leading us to a battle against those who would corrupt all we hold dear."

"As you say, but many of us think Max should continue to be our leader. We know him. What, at the end of the day, do we know about Aether. She has not been with us long and just appeared as if from nowhere," asserted Tom a seasoned lawyer by profession.

"I understand and appreciate your misgivings. But, without her, how are we to match the dark powers the star cult promotes and wishes to make our future?" countered the Duke with a touch of intolerance.

I thought carefully about leadership. Aether was already our Unicorn Queen and possessor of mighty magic. Now was the time to back her and follow her lead. Once her leadership was established, Aether ensured that her followers knew about the future they could dye for and the evil they would confront.

One evening she sought to reassure the doubters, "You now know that I have formally taken control and leadership of our mission. Hear me. I know some still have qualms about the future and, in particular, my right and suitability to fulfil that vital role. Let me assuage any doubts.

"You have witnessed at first hand my powers and how I have deployed them to protect you. That is because I am here to realise your destiny – a new world dedicated to goodness. Join with me. We can do that together."

Eventually, the army moved north again, heading for New Orkney. It was a massive logistical exercise but had been well thought through with scouting parties having plotted the way and reported back. Provisioning was demanding but planned for in advance.

They too traversed the inhospitable flow country rife with strange mutating insects and shifting boggy ground. Each day saw disease take another soul and pestilence sat on the army's shoulder like a shroud.

Unfortunately, for whatever reason, news of the flow monster had not reached them. Having barely entered this hell, and settled down for their first night, a steady thrumming shook through the heavy sphagnum moss lair they slept on by the side of the road. It was evil come to their door. Revenge it's watch word.

Aether sensed wrongdoing. The Star Masters were at work. This would be epic. The whole bog quivered for miles around. The centre parting like a volcanic eruption. The beast of the bog was gigantic with massive tentacles reaching for the camp.

It pushed aside the floating landscape before it with ease, upending the road. This beast could move mountains. The Unicorn Queen had dared to challenge it in its own territory. There would now be a reckoning with these piffling particles. And the beast was starving.

The unicorn knew this was it's time. Aether raised a hand over her head saying to her unicorn, "This abomination knows no good and has lain here beneath the bog for millennia. Fear it not. Believe me it fears you. And it should. As does part of me. Go forth and decimate."

The unicorn galloped full tilt at the seemingly astonished beast who flailed and railed. No matter how hard the beast angled it's tentacles, the unicorn floated on and on heading for the quivering maw of this giant. The single, pointed and spiralled alicorn impregnated below the beast's massive beak.

Immediately, golden light shot down every segment of the beast's structure. It was a fatal thrust. The beast shook violently and died. Calmly the unicorn retracted it's horn and padded gently to Aether's side who offered up a tender embrace in appreciation. They glowed in unison. But it was a dark glow like shimmering coal dust.

As with the Star Bringer before, Aether's army also reached the north coast. Their spies had reported back on the cult's occupation of New Orkney. This eventual location held no surprises for the Unicorn Queen. She was all too aware of the star gathering powers that had existed there forever.

Her followers now faced a real dilemma – all the boats had been taken and there were no trees to build a fleet. This seemed insurmountable. The months passed. As always, food was scarce and becoming hard to come by.

Then, one fine day, a vast armada came to anchor off port from the east. They had slid from a bank of sea mist. One moment the sea was empty and the next there was a fleet. They appeared to rest weightless on the ocean and when their oars dug into the waves they skimmed the water.

Their prows and sterns set high and topped with gilded dragons, serpents and weird and wonderful beasts. The bright, full sun glinted off the wet oar blades. Telescopes showed many armed warriors, quite a number with modern weaponry.

The lead galleon was set with red sails and the substructure was jet black. At its prow stood an elegant figure all in black studying their fortifications. Aether sensed a need to go to this strange figure and caste off, with her small crew, rowing to the battleship. She knew no fear. Her unicorn stood proud looking out to sea from the harbour wall.

As her small dinghy drew closer, so did the sheer size of this brigand cutter materialise before her.

The remote figure shouted, "Welcome travellers. We are in difficult times. And, like you, wary of strangers and what they want. Come aboard."

A rope ladder was lowered and Aether climbed to the deck. Before her was an array of warriors hard-bitten and determined. The black form appeared to float down from the quarter deck. She moved to meet Aether with a handshake. The contact was strange. This was another woman leader. And a very powerful one. Not to be underestimated.

She spoke in a strangled style of English and was clearly from foreign climes

"We are a long way from home and looking for a new land to live. Why are you here ? "

Aether thought and spoke, "Our land to the south is New Caledonia. A dark force emerged there led by a wicked Star Bringer, bent on bringing chaos to our new world. She has strange other worldly abilities. And has set up her Star Court in yonder island of New Orkney."

"And you are?"

Aether looked her straight in the eyes and declared, "Together with my followers and my unicorn, we represent the force that will ensure this evil is defeated and, in so doing, render the new world safe and fair for all."

The crew murmured.

"I am Renat the leader of this fleet. We will consider what you have said and maybe meet again."

Aether responded, "I am Aether the Unicorn Queen. We have no ships and need to get to New Orkney. If you wish to join us in our perilous quest we would combine to form a formidable challenge."

On her return, Aether had a word and I proffered, "Careful, we do not know these people and these are troubled times. There are many of them."

Aether, looking calm and authoritative, reassured, "I read it in her eyes. They surely do not trust us and they know we do not trust them. But their leader Renat knows what side to play on and Max, she will come our way. Meanwhile we wait."

Days passed and the massive fleet rested at anchor. Small dinghies were sent ashore to fill barrels with fresh water but their crews remained tight lipped and secretive. A week had passed when early one morning there was an earth shattering explosion that vibrated across the sea. They had cannons.

Aether turned and smiled at Max. She clearly was not at all surprised. A rather splendid small light craft then left the flagship, Renat resplendent at the bow.

On alighting at the pier, she strode confidently and with her retinue towards Aether declaring,

"We have considered your offer. Are interested. And now need to discuss terms and strategy. But I now make it clear I lead my crews. Nobody else. And certainly not you Aether."

At that moment, from the folds of Renat's voluminous flock coat descended a rather strange creature. Best description is probably a rather large ochre coloured rodent with startling crimson eyes. This creature just stood there on all fours surveying all before it assessing the situation. Then it turned to Aether and, in a disturbingly human voice, projected, "I am come to you Aether at the anointed hour. Evil shall not prevail whilst we are on this planet. Humans, you may call me Seeker. While I am here."

Astonishingly, Aether laid herself prostate before this Seeker.

It spoke, "I have come among you to prevail. And we shall together. If you think you understand the extent of my powers, then you don't."

All present had seen much in this odd new world but this; this was difficult to comprehend.

Those gathered on the pier and on the overlooking hillsides cheered. They sensed the latent power and energy brought their way. Last, but by far from least, the noble unicorn came forth glowing in admiration.

Stooping it's head low to the ground the Seeker stroked the unicorn's mane and lent gently to say to the unicorn and the unicorn alone, "It has been eons and light years my dear Zear since we met. What we are about to embark on will imprint our glorious greatness forever. Stay the task with me and Aether and nothing on this planet or beyond can overcome us."

Zear backed away to Aether's side. The players were in place. Aether decreed, "Let the game begin."

This was met with roars of support and feverish adulation of what they saw before them. The very air vibrated.

The Duke was not happy and wondered how much Aether would continue to seek his views given the arrival of her new companions, "My dear Aether. We have been through much together. I trust and respect you. And hope that it is reciprocal. I appreciate you know these newcomers and I do not. But I do sense a strangeness about them and around them."

"Do not feel aggrieved Duke. I will always value your companionship and strategic advice. Zear, you know and the Seeker will prove a great, and much needed, boost to our campaign."

*

Penumbra was shaking. She had not anticipated the presence of the Seeker as reported to her by her spies. The Star Sisters were one thing but the Seeker did not augur well for her mission. The Seeker was extremely dangerous with untold powers.

And it gave her cause to ponder. This was disturbing. Penumbra faltered unsure of her path for the first time. More would be needed to succeed. She opened a portal, spoke to the Star Masters and waited. And waited. Weeks passed. Her spies she had left behind at the north coast harbour of Scrabster reported back regularly on Aether's plans. Nothing could be gleaned and nothing appeared to be happening. Penumbra's paranoia grew.

Penumbra made routine inspections of her Orkney base. To encourage her troops and to ensure order. And, in a way, to reassure herself. On one such trip amongst the settlements, she was told time and time again about an old man who had just appeared a few days ago in the middle of the standing stones. There were increasing tales of him healing and he was alleged to have produced, from thin air, food and water.

Penumbra was intrigued and ordered he be brought before her to the Star Court.

And so he came with his followers in train. Penumbra knew, as soon as he stood before her, that she needed to be very wary. This could be the assassin she knew would come.

The stranger inclined his head politely saying, "You do not know me but you will. I come as a gift to aid your cause. My darkness is and will be. Whilst I am here you may call me Erebus."

The Star Bringer felt the malice creep towards her and it gave her sustenance. Her Shadow shook with pleasure. Here was someone who worshipped the star and wanted this new world bent to its knees to serve their purpose. It would not return to goodness, fairness and reason. Chaos had to reign. No compassion. No justice. Just fear and obedience subservient to the few.

Chapter 7

Orkney

Now came the task of the Unicorn Court to determine how the combined force now available to them should go about routing the star cult. Transport was available with the large fleet of armed fighting vessels. They had a large well equipped and motivated army. All led by a deadly triumvirate of the Seeker, Aether and Zear.

Aether had excluded the Duke from this process deliberately as planned, as she did not want him getting too close to her thinking. It was necessary to put up a mental and physical separation between them, lest he prove a disrupter who would have to be dealt with. The Seeker did not take prisoners.

The Duke was well aware of his gradual excommunication from planning and Aether moving away from any relationship they may have developed. It stung and he was angry but there was very little he could do about it. Planning for such a momentous undertaking would entail detailed battle planning and settling on longer term strategies.

Essentially, how to capture, how to kill and how to stay alive. The army had sworn allegiance, been comprehensively trained, knew how to use and deploy their various weapons, those selected knew how to lead and all were battle ready.

But the Duke now sensed a greater plan and began to wonder whether it was all for the good. The Unicorn Court war plan evolved. Planning not only had to take account of the operational minutiae for the battles ahead, but how the new world would be shaped once conflict was settled. Renat had used the lead time to sneak spies across the sound to New Orkney and back. What they reported back on would prove invaluable.

Meanwhile, the Star Court army had been ensconced on New Orkney for some time and were well dug in and settled. The island's rare fertile earth was being tilled and the surrounding sea was rich in fish. The army was well versed in all aspects of combat and trenchant defences were established. Any landings would encounter formidable defence mechanisms, all tainted with magic.

The channel that lay between Aether's army and New Orkney was turbulent and disturbed, with massive whirlpools ready to take to the bottom even the largest ships. Climate change had had a dramatic effect – cyclones never seen some sixty years ago were now legion. Waves could be enormous. Ships would be lost.

Thankfully, Renat's fleet were well versed in such conditions and had available excellent maritime charts enabling the campaign to have a good chance of making this short crossing with minimal loss. Two weeks passed as storms ravaged the straits. Eventually, the day came when conditions seemed settled and the flotilla set sail a few ships at a time to minimise large losses.

As in centuries past in Orkney, there were some key entry points for attacks from the sea. Many were however exposed to either Atlantic or North Sea storms. And such a large army had to have a relatively level sandy beach to stand off and to land on. Much consideration was given to this. The Star Bringer's entourage were located round the ancient Ring of Brodgar.

After much consideration it was eventually determined that the beach at Finstown, whilst not ideal, would suffice. It was on the east coast of the mainland and within striking distance of the Ring. All were sworn to secrecy as landing there, so close to their target, would account for a huge element of surprise and significantly reduce the need to take their army over extensive, difficult terrain.

Neolithic, Pictish and Viking sites were scattered across the islands – some seventy islands in all surrounding the mainland. The Ring of Brodgar, on the mainland, was five thousand years old: older than Stonehenge and the Pyramids. It is thought that, originally, there were some sixty stones: now some twenty remained. It was part of a huge ceremonial complex of standing stones and settlements and the Ring was surrounded by mounds containing neolithic tombs and bronze age burial grounds.

It had always been assumed that it had no astronomical alignment. Far from it. Little did they know. The surrounding landscape reeked of something beyond. It was an especially enigmatic and mysterious monument.

Steeped with magic. Historians referred to the Ring as the Temple of the Moon, and the nearby Standing Stones of Stenness as the Temple of the Sun. It was also suggested that the Ring was a lunar observatory. The Star Masters and Star Sisters knew exactly what it was.

The Star Bringer and the Unicorn Queen both knew that the Ring had always been a centre of control linked to a giant red star of first magnitude and some thirty seven light years away. Its name – Arcturus.

One of the brightest stars in the sky and accorded a special role in the ancient world. Shining many more times more brightly than the sun. This star was soon to show planet earth just how special it was. It had a crucial role to play in the future of the Greatness.

The first flotilla arrived and anchored a discrete distance off New Orkney. One ship in the next flotilla was less fortunate. The dramatic climate convulsions had disturbed the very fabric of the planet. What had feasted before was feasting again. It was a very rough passage and it was taking all their seamanship to weather this storm.

Sailors knew well that being at sea is to accept constant change. Conditions can shift from calm to furious without warning. You cannot fight the sea and you cannot give up. Tales of the many tentacled mythical sea monster, the kraken, floated in whispers amongst the highly superstitious sailors.

They were, as often was the case, prescient. Suddenly, and without warning, the giant tentacles embraced the very structure of the craft, squeezing. The crew looked on askance, as the decking planks popped and sundered. It did not take long. Quickly their ship started taking on water and flooding the holds. Panic reigned.

This creature, which had the appearance of a giant squid and was some sixty feet long, gorged on bodies washed into the frothing sea. Soon, all was quiet save the churning of the giant waves and the howling of the wind. As if the ship and its crew had never been.

More ships embarked for this short but dangerous crossing. Most went well. But two more ships met unexpected ends. The crossing lay at the very spot where the flow of one mighty ocean – the Atlantic Ocean met the flow of another – the North Sea.

This massive conflagration caused fearsome whirlpools which, once you got caught in their track, sucked you and your ship relentlessly and ever faster to the centre where all were dismembered and pulled down below to a salty grave. Eventually, after a couple of weeks, the whole massive fleet were anchored off New Orkney. Aether was scanning the landscape around the small fishing village of Finstown when she saw a pall of black smoke rising steadily from further inland.

Penumbra's settlement was riven with doubt about the latest development there. The severe heat and humidity was taking a heavy toll on both armies general health. The constant hot breeze cresting this flat island reduced somewhat the infestation of voracious insects. But personal and general hygiene were poor.

Close and insanitary living conditions together with an almost complete lack of medication and medically qualified clan members. A corrosive mixture where simple scratches and rashes festered and limbs and lives were lost. But worse was coming.

It started with some in the camp suffering from weakness, fatigue, diarrhoea, chills and a rash. The camp, with a couple of thousand followers, had many and varied occupations represented but only two medical doctors and a dozen nurses. It transpired, after further investigation, that it was the killer typhoid.

Food and water had the infectious bacteria in them and the infestation was spreading like wildfire. In the absence of vaccines and antibiotics, this was going to take many, especially children and intervention was needed.

Quickly measures were introduced to improve overall sanitation with particular emphasis placed on personal cleanliness, toilet protocols and water supplies. Gradually, the bacteria lost its hold.

Sadly, several hundred died. Penumbra called a meet, "This has proved a testing blow to our community and to our cause. But it was a natural calamity. You know now what we need to do to keep this disease from our homes and families. The poor children we have lost. Erebus will conduct a service to honour all we have lost. Prepare bonfires for tonight so that we might send their souls into the glorious dark."

Funeral pyres were set. With the shortage of trees, dead heather and other scrubs were added to the heaps and faggots. All were gathered. Anxious and sad, reflecting on their loss. Erebus made his grand entrance when he alighted amongst his devotees. Clothed in shimmering black that appeared to drift about his person.

Dark red hair to his shoulders and a huge golden brooch pinned to his plaid. His sword belt was leather studded with silver. While his great sword, Bone Splitter, was sheathed in leather banded with bronze strappings. His boots were of the finest soft leather, with iron plates on either side of the ankles.

Raising his gloved hand, he summoned to his side a huge dog-like an animal with a massive head. Long yellow teeth, lethal, with drool dripping from its cavernous maw. Slowly, the beast settled at the booted feet of his master looking up at him tenderly and with absolute undiminished devotion

"Behold star children, this is my dear companion – Canker. It will serve us well. Do not approach it. It is mine and mine alone. "

The beast looked out to the crowd – fear spread like ink into a blotter. Its dark presence was tangible. Groping towards their very souls. Invasive. Penetrating. Erebus continued

"Tonight has a special purpose. Yes, companions have fallen, not to our enemy, but to an abomination that knows no purpose and which maims and kills without remorse and indiscriminately. We mourn together their passing."

The hellhound Canker let forth a shattering mournful howl that vibrated for miles around.

The epidemic had hit the camp hard. Committed as they were, conditions were rough and many were having great difficulty adjusting their lives to this new world and the competing forces grappling for control.

A lady commented, "There just isn't enough food on this godforsaken island. No trees. No food. Disease. Plagues. This Erebus character is an odd one. I don't trust him. In it for himself and that weird animal. We really need to think what we are here for. Maybe we should leave."

"Yes Grace, many of us are not sure what to do now. We still support Penumbra and agree on what world she wants. But is this the way. How long before we all go up in smoke. She is supposed to have halted Armageddon but, friends, I see little sign of that. Do you?"

As evening fell, all the huge pyres were set and fired. Many souls departed upwards to the stars, their home.

Erebus incanted, "My children go to a better place where they will know pure dark and complete lack of empathy. A wonderful place amongst its fellow stars. A dark place. Cold. Unforgiving. Where there is no weakness. Stealth and lies reign supreme.

"Now my children, we have forces that are gathering near us and bent on your destruction. This is a great battle we will face together. We do not underestimate them. We are for the Star Masters and they are for the Star Sisters. You need not be too concerned with such strange forces – your world as you know it no longer exists. Now others have taken control.

"We will show you the way back. Only we can do that. Put your faith in me. I am you and you are me. Your generals and officers will begin the task of planning our campaign to make the most of our resources and manpower. The star is with you. Bring darkness."

Meanwhile, disembarkation of our massive army was no small undertaking. I had had extensive meetings with the Unicorn Court – Aether, Zear, Renat and the Seeker – to settle on the best approach to achieve an optimum landing and establishment of a base camp. Also, how best to defend and to attack. There was surprising agreement. But it was very noticeable that it was the Seeker who held and pulled the strings.

The Seeker reeked malice. It hung around him like a shroud looking for its next victim. Difficult for me to see this creature dedicated to goodness. I could not shake these doubts. They festered and fermented like a noxious cocktail, like a worm in my ear, like stone in my boot and like a blot on my soul. And the Duke was nowhere to be seen.

Fleet commanders began and orchestrated the challenge of moving all involved, plus masses of equipment and supplies, to the shore and onward to respective locations in the camp being established at the same time. Whilst, all the time, using advance parties to ensure that the dark Star Bringer got no breath of our coming and did not catch us unawares.

A forlorn hope, given the ever present possibility of spies in either camp. The landing site, which served also as base camp, was fairly level with a freshwater burn flowing into the bay, which was tidal and quite shallow. Necessitating the fleet to moor a furlong out from shore where there was sufficient draught.

This, in turn, meant a constant toing and froing using a small fleet of dinghies. They were crewed by a cluster of swarthy seamen handpicked by Renat to perform this tedious but vital task. An army marches on its stomach and provisioning was all important.

As was the need to keep an eye on possible infiltration. They were not far from their enemy and all were aware of attacks lurking like a cleaver over your head. Ships were especially vulnerable to fire as all mariners were only too aware.

Setting up the camp was a major logistical undertaking, even after thorough planning – barracks; officer's quarters; a map and planning war room; an armoury; storage facilities for food, water, ammunition and building materials; establish guard posts, watch towers and perimeter fencing; medical and dental surgeries; a unicorn chapel; an exercise and training yard; combat pit; privy, bathing and waste pits; a siege workshop with smithy and forge; redoubts trenches and stockades; kennels and graves. Such detailed planning bred healthy, well-motivated and trained troops, ready to fight much more effectively and with much greater chance of success.

Allied to this, there had been thoughtful allocation and matching of varied experiences and abilities to an efficient war machine – commanders, advisors, bodyguards, officers, elite units, scouts, rangers, watchmen, camp guards, soldiers, sailors, engineers, siege crews, dog handlers, technicians, armourers, weapon smiths, fletchers, bowyers, blacksmiths, cartwrights, cart-ographers, message runners and cooks.

Camps were the strength of the victorious, the refuge of the defeated. Sometimes, when facing defeat in the open ground armies have retreated to camp to refresh, followed by a sudden sally out to overthrow the enemy. Your camp is your second home. A tent is a soldier's home, a soldier's breath.

In pitching camp, every person knew their job without having to be told. Different parts of the camp were distinctly marked out and measured off to enable those arriving to proceed unhindered to their respective stations. The camp was, overall, made to suit the nature and contours of the ground. Most importantly, the camp occupied a defensible position with access and command to water.

I was allocated, together with the leaders, a tent in the very centre of the camp. This complex contained a series of large brightly painted tents which were rather lavishly furnished. Together with a generous supply of wine.

The supply of whisky to the army was carefully regulated to maintain order as was the oversight of the camp stills to minimise over supply and overindulgence. The Unicorn Court were sometimes less democratic in what they did, and indeed demanded, as opposed to what they advocated to their loyal disciples.

A young officer was assigned to lead a select forward command unit with very special fighting and scouting abilities. Ejan was her name. Charming but deadly. Deceptively, a languid placatory character with a keen penetrating mind allied to a keen penetrating blade. Many a man had underestimated her to their cost, sometimes fatal. She was completely fearless and had the absolute loyalty of her unit soldiers. They would die for her and did.

A real difficulty was getting hundreds of our men and women over the skyline from our camp to the enemy camp at the Ring of Brodgar without being seen too soon from the enemy's massive fortified campsite. In time, through the work of our forward scouting unit, we discovered a route shrouded by large rocks.

The officers heading up the many troops and brigades were summoned to the Unicorn Court.

Detailed plans were put before them over maps of the various approaches to the Star Bringer's extensive campsite which meandered like an octopus with tentacles all emanating from the magical mysterious Ring of Brodgar. There was much discussion. General Mulin, a former regular army general, and now in his early fifties, was concerned.

"We must get this right. Any mistakes will be heavily punished. And none of us, excepting the Court, have any understanding of magic and what part that will play on both sides. All I can do is utilise my training and experiences of fighting and the best tactics to employ for success, minimising damage and casualties on our side," emphasised the general.

"Indeed. We expect no more. Indeed, we are very proud to lead such a formidable, well provisioned efficient force. And, rest assured, we will lead your brave men and women to victory. But this will be a hard fought war. Many will fall, it will be bloody. There will be surprises and magic on both sides. When all is in the balance, that is the moment for resolve and conviction. Pushing through to win. Always being resourceful and strategic. We have prepared well," announced Aether standing proud in her tent, her silhouette shimmering on the canopy roof above the flaming brazier located at her feet.

The Seeker jumped down to the floor on to a magnificent dark red woollen carpet. Lifted his head, locked his crimson eyes on all present and, with a magical enticing cadence, declared, "Friends, there is much at play here. I come to you, and this planet, to seek redemption for what has befallen you. The evil Star Bringer promises much, not least reversing climate change. I concede it does seem so. But beware. This is just a device to reinforce her cause.

"Although a strange concept to you in this turbulent world, she represents the Star Masters an alien power beyond your imaginings. Their mission. To subvert you all to slaves under the star, a darker wicked world. My mission, and that of my revered companions, is to free your world from such tyranny and occupation.

"And to do so on behalf of the Star Sisters who have, for millennia, chased and diminished these dark forces. We will win. Let us now prepare for imminent war. A special forward unit will first test their strength, resolve, equipment and numbers. Go forth with faith. Let your unicorn light shine. We will see you through this," declared the Seeker, bowing gracefully to all and leaping back to lie on its cushion on the beautifully designed iron camp seat. A strange creature indeed. But the power, the power. It was tangible.

Chapter 8
Battle

The very capable Ejan led her select forward war party out of camp at midnight. The trek across to the Ring of Brodgar would take an estimated half a day if all went well. They had gone this way before and were confident about their plan. It was springtime in Orkney.

At their feet, they strode through meadow buttercup, flag iris, marsh marigold and wild primrose. But their eyes were not on nature: rather the prospect of being spotted by the enemy who, they knew, also had guards stationed well outside the confines of their camp. But all was quiet so far.

Suddenly, as they approached a gurgling burn, Ejan lifted her right hand. Her unit froze, statues in the darkness. Minutes passed. Then a beautiful roe deer vaulted over the burn and was gone in an instant. All that could be heard now, above the incessant flow of the burn, was the constant murmur of vastly increased insect life ever ready to deave the unwary.

They trudged on through the night, weapons at the ready. The camp had few guns, but two of the soldiers were armed and familiar with their firearms which could prove crucial should they be overwhelmed in their planned initial exploratory foray. The rest of their approach went well, without any further frights. But there was real deep seated fear. They knew this was very risky.

They heard and smelled the enemy camp before they saw it.

Ejan whispered, "Be ready. They may be and if they are, comrades, then be ready to retreat very quickly at my command."

And so it proved. The unit had just crested the last small hillock moving stealthily, when they were met by a highly organised defensive unit armed and ready. Battle for most was a hammering rage, a killing orgy. Three wedges formed quickly in front of our advancing line.

The enemy stood tightly packed like silver herrings in a barrel, shields of iron, steel and wood with the rear rank holding their shields directly over their helmeted heads. When composed, their leader tapped his shield and they advanced on Ejan's unit at a steady pace, cheering and jeering. They had time to think about what they faced and their fate.

There were a couple of archers to the rear and they loosed their bows, the shimmer of feathers glistening in the early morning light as the arrows arched, deceptively innocently, towards our unit. This took its toll. Then came the spears. Still, many of our small unit survived as our two, strategically placed, shooters started to target their oncoming ranks.

Bows were surprisingly useful as they kill at a great distance and, even if they do not kill or maim, they make an enemy nervous. Going into volleys of arrows is a blind business and keeping behind your shield was critical.

Even after just the initial foray, the heather and grass was slick with blood and bodies lay strewn and splayed on the ground. Ejan licked the blood from the long shaft of her spear and gave a sly smile. The initial carapace formation had proved difficult at first to impregnate.

But such was the resolve, bravery and ingenuity of the unit soldiers, that the structure was quickly broken apart and the killing began. Ferocious hand to hand slaying. One of theirs was still resisting doggedly and with no little skill. A worthy opponent who demanded respect.

Alert, fit and made to fight. He faced our foraging unit, huge in cloak and heavy leather, reinforced with plate. He spread his arms as though crucified and, in his calloused hands, was a massive battle double sword, wielding it as if it was a feather.

He was terrifying – a big man, snarling, eyes wild, hair dripping red with flecks of blood. Ejan bounded straight at him completely fearless. They clashed like a thunderbolt. The very ground shook as they strained for footing, lunging and thrusting.

She was much shorter and his great blade pummelled and battered relentlessly. Then, he tripped going backwards over a corpse. It was enough. Ejan darted in, thrusting her dagger in below his shield and armour twisting and probing. It was fatal and he slumped, felled like a giant oak.

Ejan sensed more troops rushing out of the campsite and

yelled for retreat. The riflemen guarded their backs, sniping as they went. It just gave enough time to head for the hills. Some of the unit were outpaced and brought down under a reign of blades, chopping and hacking. Ejan shuddered as she leapt over the burn. The unit lost many in the end. There would be a reckoning.

Later that day, Ejan stood before the Unicorn Court still reeling from the rout and the loss of so many.

Aether was first to put her arm round her, commiserating for the fallen and saying, "You all fought bravely. It was a difficult mission and, as expected, you took casualties. It was important to gauge our enemy and we have tested and tasted their metal."

"Yes, at a cost. But war it is. They have a massive spread out camp site set out in what, at first sight, looks rather random and higgledy piggledy. But, on closer scrutiny, I determined a bastion defence outline reaching out from the centre in a star like formation, to afford maximum opportunity to assault enemies coming from different directions.

"Outside this main fortification were ditches of varying depths. But we could not see what lay at their base. For example, whether they contained wooden spiked posts to impale our troops. At the perimeter there were stone barriers, interspersed with elevated guard posts," offered Ejan carefully. Many had fallen for this precious information.

"Thank you Ejan and your unit. The Star Court will now assess this and determine how best, and when, to launch an all-out assault," added Aether.

All through that night, and throughout the next two days, the Unicorn Court deliberated. This war must be won and great care was needed to not only win but reduce those they fought to a rump that would never again threaten the new world. A plan was hatched and then presented to the officers to consider and implement, in consultation with their troops and all their helpers. This took a further day.

Our army consisted of some three thousand fighting troops in total. Most armed with swords, daggers, spears and war axes. With just a hard core of a few hundred fully trained and familiar with battle. Much though had been picked up in their eventful travels north and the skirmishes they had lived through. Within this cadre, there were specialists – archers and shooters.

And groups assigned specific roles and tasks – forward elite units who would divide and intimidate, others would supply bridging and laddering over ditches and other barricades, a small deadly group of shooters with rifles and scopes assigned to take out quickly commanders and key players, archers to drive their shafts deep into the enemy compound and, last but not least, the doughty foot soldiers to charge, harry and cleave the oncoming hordes.

A giant Meet was called. The Unicorn Court seated on a hillock, looking down on the assembled multitude. The spokeswoman was Aether. Her unicorn Zear at her side as always

"Friends. Together we will prevail. Do not doubt it. We are well prepared and the light shines eliminating the dark. You are that light. It is in your right hand – starlight. Look at your Court. Special, very special. Whatever the dark ones bring to the battle, we will more than match it. So do not falter, do not fear. A new world beckons. "

The Seeker unfolded its tiny frame from its favourite comfy chair, leapt on to the back of Zear, and magically projected it's voice across the gathered. This was a different voice, laced with power and confidence. A voice that seduced with its superiority and calm conviction

"We go to war tomorrow. You all now know what to do, how and when. I leave details to others. What I will produce, with your help, is complete and utter victory. Yes, we will win. Tomorrow, I will be amongst you. You will not fight alone. The whole Unicorn Court will join in the heat of battle. Our light will spread to support your light. Darkness will be vanquished."

Duke took the opportunity to sidle up to Aether. He had, in earlier times, felt he had a special close relationship with her. But, since the arrival of these magical beings, he had sensed a distance growing between them, "Aether, I am confident our forces will prevail. But it could be a close call. I am not sure we know what we might face. War does not determine who is right, only those who are left.

You can believe all you like but that does not set the outcome. Wars almost always never end the way starters had in mind. So, Aether we must be sure of our strategy and using our army to maximum effect."

"Well said Duke. It is good to hear your wisdom again. Let me put your concerns to bed – considerable care and thought has been given to our war plan and any magical capacity they can deliver is well outmatched by ours. Be safe my friend and let the light protect you," reposted Aether as diplomatically as possible.

In darkness that night the army moved out. They did so on a broad front and at staged timings. The objective was to surround the enemy camp and strike as one from all quarters, fragmenting their forces and disrupting their defence plans.

Much pivoted on not being spotted on the approach. Heather and bracken had been cut and were used as camouflage as the massed regiments crawled slowly and carefully to surround the diverse parts of the camp. This was a tedious patient task, well worth the effort. Eventually, some were spotted and the alarm went up. All hell broke loose. A cacophony of sound mixing shouts, groans, clash of steel, thud of shield on shield, shouting of orders, thunder of feet, crack of bone and squelch of blades into flesh.

Eventually, my time came to join the fray unfolding before me. A bloody sight indeed. I had slung my sword – Honour Light – on my back as it is easier to draw in the heat of battle and the very first, and vital, stroke is a hard downward hack. In my right hand was my short stabbing dagger – Light Touch – made for eviscerating at close quarters.

There was much blood in the air, screaming and then a sword lunged from my right going between my shield and body. Instinctively, I kicked back deflecting the first thrust. A second jab followed, nicking my right hand. I was moving slowly now through the seething steaming mass of bodies. The flash of blades, the clash of steel. the gurgle of death, the stink of defecation, the smell of fear all permeated – a noxious roiling poultice.

With no cure but to fight on. I recall crouching as I thrust ahead, the huge axe blade descending and raised my shield and deflected the stroke, my arm shuddering and shaking. Next, I fell over a horse corpse, leaving myself vulnerable. And so it proved, as a star disciple tried to gut me with a short blade only to be stopped by the belt buckle around my waist.

The blade came at me as if in slow motion, striking my belt. Seizing the dagger hilt, I turned it, forcing the cold steel up his thigh ripping his muscles and ripping open blood vessels terminating in his groin.

I thought he was gone but, somehow, his sword slammed into my shield again, skidded across the wood and skittered past my head. I danced backwards and he charged again, hoping to pin me with his weight in his death throes.

He lunged, I deflected, noting the river of blood running down both his legs.

Surely, he would fail soon. I kept him turning to tire him out as he swung into empty air. Mud was everywhere so I had to take care. Still he threatened with that massive sword. I suddenly switched my blade to my other left hand. It worked. He hesitated. I struck low and fast, finding my target at last. Then he fell. Dead.

The Duke had earned his fighting credentials on the rugby fields of Eton and in shoots where he dispatched pheasants and grouse from butts. Now he was in the new world, surrounded by a seething mass of humanity hell-bent on ripping him apart. When pressed he showed his metal. He was no soft bellied fop.

His elite education had also enabled him to train and learn how to deploy an epee. A weapon similar to a foil but heavier, with a larger guard and a much stiffer blade. It was a thrusting sword and the Duke was its master, thrusting and stabbing to deadly effect. Many fell before his terrifying onslaught.

Meanwhile, the battle raged. Like a giant fermentation, the battle boiled and seethed. Almost as if two giants were intent on carnage and destruction. The battle ploughed on uninhibited. There was clever strategic resistance with the specialist units on both sides eroding each other's capabilities. A real war of attrition. Inside this seething cauldron of human flesh the soldiers fought for their lives.

Thrusting, gasping, wailing, grasping, yielding, slipping, sinking, praying – an unholy hymn of individual and collective suffering. Slowly, very slowly, our army gained the upper hand, pushing forward across the armed ditches and dykes. A steady slog of death and daring. But we were winning. And so the carnage continued unabated.

This was the very first time many of the foot soldiers had fought, let alone in deadly, face to face, combat. The ground, covered in bog myrtle, was now soaked in piss and blood. Then it happened. An ominous swathe of darkness swept over our army, obliterating all it fell on. Erebus had entered the fray. The response from Aether was stunning, a shard of brilliant light seemingly eradicating Erebus as if he had never existed.

Our troops cheered in the middle of the melee. The enemy were wrong footed. Our troops stepped up their attack and reached the outskirts of the camp on all sides. What could now hold them back. They had not long to wait. Penumbra now knew what she had to do.

She knew she could call down more power from her Masters, using the Ring to amplify her capacity. Just then a black torrent of evil cascaded from the heavens, forming a spout of blackness burrowing into the very centre of the Ring of Brodgar.

Penumbra sucked in to her that blackness and let loose a spike of raw malice at Aether. It never reached her. Instead, it alighted on the Unicorn's spiralled alicorn and was readily subsumed as if it had been nothing. Penumbra was flustered, a rare event, and ordered a retreat. The armies parted.

The Seeker shone like a star, light emanating from his small carcass in every direction. All turned to the light, like moths to a fire. He held all before him in suspension and a state of wonder, including Penumbra. This was impressive, really impressive.

It spoke, "Listen. I can obliterate everyone here without effort or conscience. Believe it. So, I offer you the star followers a choice – death or unconditional surrender to the light side. Your choice." It waited, the crimson eyes glowing in anticipation. Then, it commanded those still against to the right – several hundred sidled there."

It licked it's thin lips languidly with a black narrow tongue. And then, like lightening, decimated all those who chose death. Noticeably, Penumbra had not moved.

Then Erebus struck, his hellhound Canker heading straight for the Seeker. How Erebus had survived was not clear. Canker was huge, biting and chomping his deadly run through the troops. Bullets were, weirdly, deflected with casual disdain. The diminutive Seeker stood firm as Canker bore down on it.

Canker had his massive drooling maw ready to consume this little creature in front of him. The Seeker merely looked at Canker who froze on the spot. Ruthlessly, Canker's massive head was parted from its frozen body, clunking on to the ground and melting away quickly in the heat.

The rage emanating from Erebus echoed eerily across the fighting fields as he cut a bloody random swathe through both armies. He was incandescent. The Seeker would fall; so he thought. When in sight and closer range, Erebus brought forth a massive black creature some thirty feet in height.

It buzzed with menace and sought to envelop the Seeker who quickly disappeared inside it. A few seconds passed, then an almighty implosion as this monster was ripped apart. The Seeker was ejected gently. Erebus and his monster had gone. Forever.

Turning casually, the Seeker placed white cords round Penumbra and ordered she be incarcerated. Her fate would come. Not to be rushed. An example would be set. Sheepishly, and supplicant, those who had chosen light had the stars seared from their foreheads to be straight away replaced by a unicorn emblazoned on their right hand.

All then bowed in absolute devotion to the Seeker. How this was achieved, I know not. But achieve it, it did. Remarkable indeed. But I did wonder at what such power might bring about if possessed by the wicked and those opposing our objectives. It felt that here before me was a force but was it good or bad. Still, we had won.

It took a full day to clear the battleground. And the dead would need to be buried quickly to prevent putrefaction. It was also important to recognise their bravery, having died for their clan. The dead and dying enemy soldiers were burnt without ceremony, the cries of the still living piercing the campsite as their skin parted company from their bodies. Truly ruthless and heartless. Only adding to my doubts about our so called victory.

That evening our brave army dead were honoured, sacrificed to the light on funeral pyres and afforded respectful recognition of their honour and allegiance. The Unicorn Court, convened once again by their glorious Unicorn Queen Aether, determined to move their base camp to this new location at the Ring of Brodgar.

This took some few days. The army was now an odd mixture of the unicorn brigades and those from the dark side now converted to the light by the mysterious Seeker. But all bent to the task. The light had won the day and the Unicorn Court ruled absolutely.

On the very crest of success, the Seeker spoke to his Court, "My role here is done. Aether will take the light forward on this planet."

It then leapt into the air and vanished. Astonishing. Never seen again on planet Earth. Erebus was extinct but the Seeker no doubt still had a part to play in the great game of light and dark. Before the Seeker disappeared, it had seen our followers select their own jury to put Penumbra on trial.

The trial only lasted a couple of hours. She showed no contrition, claimed that the real danger to us was our Star Sisters and that we would rue the day they followed Aether. Strangely, what she said had a scintilla of truth in it – once again.

But all was going well for us. Once we established our cause in Orkney, we could spread the light further in this new world. Still, I had doubts. That Shadow around Aether might have got darker. The white cords, secured around Penumbra by the Seeker, held tight no matter what she incanted. The verdict was unanimous. Guilty. To be burnt as a devil dark witch at the stake. And so it was done straight away. As the flames caressed her, the Shadow sought to save her.

The bindings held tight, cutting into her as the heat increased, eventually severing her body in multiple areas. She burnt and burnt. And whispered her last, "To my Masters I now go. May the darkness devour you all."

Chapter 9
Star Born

A central part of our new settlement was the Ring of Brodgar and, at the very centre of the Ring, had been placed the royal Stone of Destiny which we had brought from its ancestral home in Perth. The Stone now stood erect and proud. All who passed, placed their right hand on the Stone and a small part of the star light from their imprinted unicorn imbued itself into the Stone. Which shone ever brighter as the months went by, through winter, and into spring.

Renat, leader of the fleet and custodian of the Seeker had, throughout the tumult, kept a careful eye on her ships which were still moored off Finstown. She didn't know where the Seeker had gone. Before his departure, it had thanked Renat for caring and transporting it. And asked her to support Aether and Zeal whatever actions they took. That summer was a time of relaxation for the camp on the back of their hard won victory.

Now it was time to enjoy and live a little. And try to come to terms with their very different new lives in this odd new world. Still, things could have gone much worse. They could eat and drink and they could love. And they had shelter.

They were still plagued by a voracious insect life and simple wounds could prove fatal. The importance of clean water and hygiene was recognised and, generally followed, so deaths were few and there were no epidemics.

It was also a great opportunity to explore their island home, using the fleet to reach the many smaller islands surrounding them. The topography of Orkney was unique. The meeting of land and sea at the coast, and the features so formed, produced the many key elements in the landscape. Not least, spectacular cliffs sculpted into arches, stacks, coastal clefts and blowholes.

The main island, and the groups of islands to both the north and south of the mainland, were predominantly low lying with gentle relief, the smooth contours of which were emphasised by the scarcity of trees and woodland cover. The landscape, though severely windswept, supported areas of arable and pasture lands. The lower areas were captive to shallow lochs and bays.

The legacy of past generations was evident in the rich archaeology of the Orkney landscape. Significantly, some of this stood upstanding after the passage of thousands of years. The Ring was an outstanding example of this. It sat at the heart of neolithic Orkney which, together with the Standing Stones of Stenness, presented an almost theatrical effect at either side of the Ness of Brodgar. All within a low lying basin surrounded by hills.

Of particular use were the rocks of Orkney. In the absence of trees for a wood supply for building, the rocks proved ideal for construction. The readily accessible rocks, especially the bedded flagstones, provided a first class building material. It's splitting properties, into slabs and blocks, facilitated the construction of homes – for walls, roofing, flagstone floors and dykes.

There were, throughout the islands, populations surviving. Some had come to join in the great battle and some had arrived to trade and barter. The extensive travel throughout the isles increased the number of useful contacts and overall collaboration with the wider community.

There was tangible fear and superstition was rife. Especially about what we were all doing there and, not least, the weird leadership figures we had, complete with an astonishing unicorn. No wonder they wondered. But they knew full well we could help them to survive and that we could help each other.

Community inclusion was important, not least to maximise the resources the islands could provide. In particular, peat extraction. In the absence of coal, peat was essential for life. It was used for heating and cooking. It was made into coke for forging iron and peat dust was used in stone masonry.

As was the tradition, the surface turf was removed and the peats cut with a special cutting tool known as a tairsgeir. With a forged iron blade almost at right angles to its wooden handle, the peat cutter could slice regular blocks of the organic soil and then they were laid out. The peat was then turned and heaped as it dried. In rows known as storrows or piled up into heaps called astorrows.

Then transported to our camp where it was stacked at convenient locations, especially the camp kitchen. Although a scorching summer, that didn't hinder overmuch the release and relief all felt in their now well established and ordered camp site.

The followers were getting to know each other and there were many marriages, with a good number expecting a child. A community was forming and there was a growing feeling of optimism in the air.

The camp had a spread of talents. At the many celebrations,

usually in the evening and going on well into the night, there were marvellous musicians, singers, dancers, poets and acrobats. Many were nights to remember and linger on in the memory.

There were, of course misdemeanours – drinking and gambling that got out of hand. The Court was strict, ever conscious of the need to maintain discipline. Offenders were punished.

Somewhat ironically, Zear was heard admonishing a rather pathetic offender, "My man, don't you know by now that you need rules and they must be applied fairly. Without rules, we are just animals."

In the middle of one such evening's raucous festivities, Aether took my hand and led me gently towards the centre of the camp. I confess, I was a little taken aback as she had never ever touched me before. But, that said, there is no doubt that trust, understanding and, yes, affection had developed between us. We reached the Stone of Destiny. She then spaced us at arm length, reaching over the Stone. We faced each other, arms stretched out towards each other. The Stone then pulsated as if alive.

Then a tremendous pulse of white energy shot up our arms. Interestingly, it was a wonderful warm feeling. Aether looked at me at that moment, almost pleading for forgiveness. Her reclusive Shadow dissipated momentarily. Then it happened. A truly magical event. Suddenly, a beautiful young woman was just there, standing on the Stone.

Aether looked lovingly into my eyes saying, "This is our child. She is the Star Born. She is called Airna."

This was miraculous. A daughter. I had witnessed power and magic. But to create, call down, a person was something else. I couldn't help but feel this was a desperate attempt by Aether to shed the shackles controlling her every move.

And that the Stone of Destiny placed here had afforded her that unique opportunity. Airna stood atop the Stone naked, as if a newborn. Quickly, Aether offered her a hand and led her away. I saw no Shadow on Airna and sensed some profound outcome for us all at the hands of this incarnation.

Airna settled in unobtrusively, with little curiosity shown by the camp. Surprisingly. Meanwhile, it did feel like the climate tsunami might have been moderating. Temperature takings confirmed this was so but only by fractions. At that rate, it would take eons to get back to levels enjoyed in the 1960s. Who could say how long and how it would end.

But there was light and it seemed to be pushing back the dark. As the first autumn approached for the camp, all was going well. No one from the decimated south had landed on any of the Orkney Islands. Not surprising. But it reinforced the likelihood of their complete annihilation and obliteration.

Following the sudden appearance of the Star Born amongst them, there continued to be a muted response, so inured to the magic they had seen on so many occasions and Airna's miraculous conception continued, for the most part, unnoticed. I was overwhelmed. A daughter. And so, life skittered along at the camp, integrating closer and closer to the Orkney folks.

The heat was easing very, very, gradually. But disease was ever present, exacerbated by the lack of doctors and dentists – only one dentist and five doctors – backed up by a smattering of nurses. Insect life continued to wreak havoc unabated. In spite of this, spirits were high and the population increased steadily. There was a genuine sense of optimism and a belief that things were getting better. Two more years passed peacefully and productively.

Zear and Aether had been considering for some time at what

stage a select party of companions should be sent south to establish what was happening there and to explore possibilities for expanding their community. And so it was that they determined who should go. They insisted I lead this motley crew. I was taken aback. To be parted from Aether and Airna. Then, to my complete surprise, Aether took my hand once again, looking me in the eye, and whispered in my ear, "My dear Max. You will be missed. I will miss you. But go you must. And take our daughter with you."

There was an immutable hint of profound unfathomable sadness emanating from her. She did not have complete control. Something else did. Zear rarely contributed but, meaningfully, offered up a significant insight of its mysterious origins, "When all is said and done Max, you and all living things on this doomed planet, are merely the incarnation of a great seething, scrambling, time travelling cooperative of viruses. I come from the stars. My state is one you cannot comprehend."

The make-up of this mission of a band of brothers and sisters was vital. A balance had to be struck between an effective mission group and leaving the camp properly defended and serviced. It was a relatively shallow pool to select from so great care was taken. Max and Airna to head it up, with Max as their leader. A medic was needed and a cook. With a small fighting unit. Renat would remain with the fleet and had allocated a ship and crew for the journey.

The doctor, John, was a modest unprepossessing character that the less discerning just didn't notice. But what a doctor, with considerable hospital specialist skills and general practice experience. Just what was needed, as he would undoubtedly be needed in the days and months ahead.

His dry sharp sense of humour would lighten dull moments as would his keen understated ability to size up people and situations instantly. A good competent reliable and intelligent man to have in your team and backing you. An all round professional.

The cook, Nigel, was a character. Loud and mouthy, given to bursting into song. He dyed his hair red and had cultivated a long thin beard. Which he oftentimes jested was used to stir the soup. At least it was hoped it was a joke. His clothes were loud. And, moreover, he sometimes adopted a dress. But what a cook. Taking great pride in his table. Woe betide any person who criticised his work – his ladles had other uses. An asset.

The fighting unit was at the very heart of the mission. The camp had two machine guns and quite a number of rifles and handguns. The decision was made to allocate one of the very precious machine guns to the mission. It was a squad automatic weapon, chambered for small calibre assault rifle ammunition and operated by one soldier. And that soldier had been a fully trained army machine gunner. The weapon and 'Andy the Gun' were as one.

Many joked that he paid more attention to his gun, constantly cleaning and assembling it, than to any woman. But Andy handled this gun to deadly effect. His role could prove crucial. This was backed up by a dozen warriors – six men and six women – half fully armed with automatic rifles and handguns.

There were also three archers and three archeresses. All six excelled at their craft. Archery was a hard taskmaster. The shiver of delight as one watched your arrows cut through the air and land just where you wanted it to. The soothing feeling soon became an addiction.

Care and maintenance of the bow was crucial – to be kept dry, avoid knocks and damage, store in as cool a place as possible to prevent moisture build up and warping or mould and, if possible, carry in a hard case. The bow had to be wiped down with a soft cloth to remove dirt and debris after use. Also, the application of wax to the bowstring to protect it from weather conditions and maintain its tensile strength. One archer, the lead archer, called Lorraine, was also a skilled fletcher who could create bows and arrows. This unit was impressive.

The ship's carpenter, affection-ately known as Woody, was crucial on a wooden ship. Woody was a skilled woodworker with shipwright experience. He was responsible for repairing damage and plugging leaks. He was also directly accountable for securing the water stocks and fire protection and drills whilst at sea.

The foot soldiers were a doughty bunch of misfits led by a lady called Bethsheba, an imposing, tall, elegant figure who was exceptionally fleet of foot and absolutely deadly with her rapier having trained in Paris. She had long blonde hair to her shoulders, wore a leather vambrace on her fighting right arm, had a scarlet red diagonal sash with scabbard and slim pointed daggers down the side of her soft black calf boots. The very epitome of a killing machine. Lovely, but once you engaged with her the die was caste and your fate sealed. Truly formidable.

And finally, the Duke. He had baulked at first, not wanting to be parted from Aether who he loved. But Aether insisted his strategic nouse was needed and asked him to take on the special role of guardian to our daughter. The Duke was a valuable addition, providing the glue to gel the group and maximise their potential. He was a reluctant passenger though.

That night they left camp, to loud cheering and well wishing. All were keen to start as soon as they knew their mission was on and they were the ones to go. It didn't take long to reach Finstown and the lighters were there to row the mission out to their awaiting ship. Captained by a burly swarthy man with tattoos all over his face resembling coiled snakes.

As he strangled this unholy visage into a smile, the serpents appeared to slither all over it. He came well recommended from Renat, was named Captain Tatum and went by the handle of Tatters.

His crew would follow him to the bottom and were the best seasoned mariners.

That night their ship pulled up anchor. It was a wonderful starlit night. And there is no better place to view the heavens than in a boat out at sea. The super bright star Arcturus shone especially brightly as if pointing the mission towards its destiny.

The mission team and crew were chatting, getting to know each other and preparing to get a night's sleep. A waxing gibbous moon above was distributing it's diluted light over this vast post-apocalyptic seascape before us. Like a luminous eye casting it's silver gaze upon this strange new world.

Sunrise was odd in this new world. The ferocious heat

worldwide cast a semi-permanent skein over the sky. This came and went with tumultuous un-predictable winds, gales and hurricanes. Although they were in the tiny part of the planet still remaining that was not totally decimated, it was a real challenge to survive, especially on the heated oceans.

The morning sun percolated as if through a sieve, cascading in rivulets across the deck and through the rigging. There was a steady breeze and the sails thrummed as the ship ploughed south. All were in good spirit and the breakfast had gone well.

Chores were tackled and there was always much to do. A night and a day shift. The night shift would handle trimming the ship and keeping it sailing. The day shift managed most maintenance, alongside keeping the ship sailing.

Pumping out the bilge was done often, sometimes as much as four or five times a day and could last quite a while. Maintaining the ropes was also a constant task. Stoning the decks, using a pumice to get rid of splinters was also common. Swabbing the decks was used to keep them damp although the humidity did aid this. Water caused wood to swell and that kept them watertight.

When an anchor had to be laid or raised, that was a huge undertaking involving many of the crew. Also, the scraping and repainting of the irons, the ship's metalwork.

The few cannon needed to be maintained. Fishing was also a common task, to help stored food last longer. And if it was raining, collecting and storing the rainwater. Added to which the furling and unfurling of sails and constantly keeping watch.

When fighting was imminent, preparing the ship was a very intense job. Officer's quarters had to be dismantled and all walls and furnishings taken below decks. Boats had to be lowered and rigged for towing. Gun decks had to be cleared and everything stowed away securely. Guns had to be unlimbered and run out.

Soldiers had to get their weapons and prepare for close quarter combat. Sick bay patients had to be moved below decks and the emergency surgery set up.

By day end the ship – *Light Bringer* – had made good progress in a steady westerly. Crews were about to change over when the crow's nest lookout signalled a heavy squall closing fast. Huge swells rolled, their white horse tips licking hungrily at the straining timbers. More was to come. With frightening speed, the waves grew in size and volume.

Looking out from the decks all one could see was this mass of water, many feet high, and well above the level of the decks, rushing as if to engulf all before it, only to go under the boat as the ship heaved and rose over them.

Suddenly, the mast swayed it's shrouds parting. Tatters bellowed out his orders over and above the boom of the waves. I yelled, but in the deafening cacophony no one could hear me. The main mast faltered and shredded, falling on to the deck. The sea poured in. The crew lifted the mast, dragged it and got it over the side cutting ropes and rigging as they went.

As quickly as it had come so did the fierce storm pass. The sea settled as if unaware of the carnage it had let loose on our dear ship. The professional crew got to work quickly but a new mast was now required and that meant striking for landfall. We limped along for the next few days in calm waters. Eventually, we managed and headed west to the mainland.

As evening approached, we headed for the small harbour at Lossiemouth, a former well known fishing village. Bethsheba was pleased, "I am not used to sailing on the high seas and a spell ashore will be very welcome for many of us. A big cheer for the crew who saw us through."

"We will see worse as the heat increases to the south. The sea is agitated and takes no prisoners. You are right to fear it, Bethsheba. The sea does not reward those who are too anxious, too greedy or too impatient. It has some potent power to make us think things we like to think. Whatever we lose, it's always ourselves we find in the sea," were the wise words from their seasoned captain Tatters.

Less their topmast, the crew navigated *Light Bringer* skilfully through the narrow harbour entrance shadowing the many craft that had gone before. The crew were on edge in these extreme times. Crew members jumped on to the harbour side with thick hawsers secured to the ship's irons, with the hawser secured to bollards and rings on the pier side. They had an audience. A small number of very curious locals. I decided we should all stay on board that night and go forth in the morning. Guards were set on the ship and ashore. The night went peacefully.

Early in the morning a gaggle of traders, selling a wide variety of goods, were spread out along the pier.

Airna addressed our crew, "Careful. We do not know what we face. There are many desperate people in desperate times. There is no law and order. We want to avoid confrontation and drawing attention to ourselves. Neither should we indicate what we are doing or, indeed, where we have come from. You will be pushed. Guard your tongues. "

The crew, fully armed, went forth to explore this village and its environs. It was important to find out what was happening. They were all quizzed. Everywhere they sensed a depressed population seemingly incapable of getting to grips with all the changes they faced. More a resignation to their fate.

Overall, a sad sight. A strong fighting force had passed through some while ago, heading north. They had been ruthless, seizing precious grain supplies and slaughtering the few beasts that had survived in the dreadful heat and disease. Some had been armed with handguns and rifles.

Money no longer had value so the crew bartered and exchanged for fresh water, salted fish and other sundries. Care was taken by all with invitations for drink and company politely declined. That night on board discussion centred on the state of the people, the armed gang and how long to remain moored here. Lorraine had heard there may be some old masts available in some of the yards.

"We now have sufficient provision to set to and stay at sea for at least a week. Personally, I think it may be prudent to seek more before we depart. And it would seem possible to do that without upsetting too much the village core supply. We know not what lies ahead," offered up Nigel the cook.

Lorraine interjected, "I agree that this would appear to be a safe temporary haven where we could not only amass intelligence but explore the surrounding area carefully."

The consensus was to stay for a week. The priority was a new mast and tomorrow contact would be made with the boat building yards. A ready to use mast would have been a great boon.

Next morning plans were hatched to secure any main mast available. But first, Woody had to work out the precise extent of the storm damage to the mast which was a complex piece of equipment. The mast was in three sections – lower mast, topmast and topgallant mast. The lower mast rested on the kelson of the ship, on a block of wood known as the step.

It passed through holes in each deck, known as the partners, and was held rigid by means of wedges.

This bottom part of the mast was made of several pieces of timber carefully joined together and secured with iron bands. Woody declared this part of the mast sound, to much relief.

The storm had however sundered the topmast, the mere splintered stump of which was still interlocked to the lower mast. The remainder of the mast having to be cut loose and heaved overboard during the storm. A new topmast and topgallant mast were required and to be fitted.

Woody commented, "Could have been worse, but much to be done and I will need as much help as possible. It may take some time and perhaps we should consider asking for any specialists available in the village. If we can trust them."

No ready-made masts appeared. The two new masts now required were made with two single pieces of timber. The topmast was attached semi permanently to the top front of the main mast and the topgallant mast secured to the top front of the topmast to enable the quick lowering in the event of heavy winds.

Airna announced, "Now we know just what we need and we have the means to do the job. Good. You know which unit is yours and what we want. Get to it."

The units eased out through the throng on the pier, spreading the word and moving round the area. There was a small shipyard and it was run by an old craggy codger sea dog called Riggy who lived boats and ship building. It was his life, his passion. And boy oh boy did he know his craft.

The *Light Bringer* was a large vessel and Riggy was not aware of any ready-made mast sections that would do the job, either lying around or part of a decommissioned ship. So, it looked as if two new mast sections would need to be crafted. Indeed, that was confirmed that evening when the units returned.

Next day, the hunt was on to get the right bits of wood. Large timbers were eventually located that would serve and were taken aboard. Riggy and Woody started, opening up their tried and tested tool bags. It was hard and exacting work, not helped by the heat and flies.

The wood had to be correct for the job. It was sitka spruce which had long been prized by spar makers for its long, clear lengths, light weight and impressive strength for that weight. The wood was dry and the grain vertical.

The days passed uneventfully. The master carpenters were nearly done shaping the new masts. The local blacksmith was due to deliver the linking ironwork and clasps. So, the day came and all gathered to raise the masts.

Airna stood before the crew, "A job well done. We can now ready the *Light Bringer* for setting sail. But let us first tarry here a few more days to explore the village hinterland. Tonight we celebrate, extra tots of whisky all round."

That night, around two o'clock, when the crew were sound asleep, the attack came. Word had got to the brigands, who had ravaged the village before, and they were now out for rich plunder, maybe even gold. There were many. They slithered up the side and over the bulwarks like giant black spiders. The alarm was raised by Bethsheba who was, fortunately, still awake and alert.

She was first on deck, dealing death to the black shrouded shapes that surrounded her. Shots rang out. A foot soldier was down, in a pool of blood. Two more followed in quick succession. It was carnage. And looking grim.

Andy the Gun had, once his head cleared in panic, set up his machine gun behind the transom wall at the stern of the ship. He quickly had clear line of sight across the deck. But the hand to hand battle raged and neither he nor other shooters could open fire.

So the fight ensued. Airna was standing back for now, not wishing to display her powers if possible. She did not want to lose more of her crew and had, discretely, eliminated their two shooters who had suddenly choked to death.

I strode into the melee, unsheathing from my back mounted scabbard my trusted blade 'Honour Light' ready for combat. Many of the usurpers were seasoned campaigners, agile, well-armed and bent on victory. They were determined, having vanquished many before. And skilled fighters. A hatchet grazed my head as I took on this small, gnarled, runt of a man who moved like lightening. His following sword thrust cut into my side and I staggered backwards scrambling for a foothold.

He pressed with another ferocious hatchet strike. I fell on the deck and it missed. He rushed on meeting the point of my upthrust sword point, lingering in astonishment on the tip before sliding slowly down the blade. I was pinned beneath his carcass. Over to my right I could just see the Duke in full flow, taking one of the enemy after another to the happy hunting ground. He was indeed a sight to behold.

Bethsheba also thrust and jabbed relentlessly, taking all before her like a dervish. Her rapier dripped with blood. Her visage serene and comforting, with a hint of mild amusement. The captain was furious at this invasion of his craft, his scimitar scything them down like ripe wheat. Disciplined, efficient, taken early and without compunction. The deck now ran with blood, oozing out through the scuppers.

Then they retreated, some diving off the deck and others clambering down the sides. Airna called a halt. Before the brigands could contrive to send fire arrows at their ship, Tatters commanded that they set sail immediately.

In short order, they were on the high seas and clear from danger. John was tending the two shot but they were both badly wounded. Luckily, I only had a flesh wound. The *Light Bringer* ploughed on through the night, the waves tipped with starlight.

The Star Masters and Sisters had played a good game so far. Looking on at their confected battle between the light and the dark was fun and great entertainment. Soon their ace card would be played to give the game a real buzz. The Watchers needed to be fed on a regular basis. They were forever hungry for stimulation.

Weary of what their universes offered up to them and, although perpetually sated and bloated, they were never ever satisfied. Always thirsting for the ultimate high, the most decadent, the most degrading, the darkest game to play. Manipulation was one of the best games and destroying goodness was truly epic and superb gameplay.

Aether and Zear were also growing weary with these dull humans in the Orkney settlement. Aether always knew that it was Zear who was the senior partner here, "It is time to move on Aether and complete our stay on this planet. As you know, we have many other worlds to explore and corrupt. The Watchers will always watch. Not just for entertainment but to ensure, through facilitators like us, that their insatiable curiosity is constantly fed. To fail them is to no longer exist," mused Zear.

"Just so Zear. Let us put the next stage into place. Tonight, will fit our purposes. Then we leave here and this planet forever. Thank goodness, it is just so drab and primitive. "

Evening came. Zear and Aether had called a Meet and the followers were placed all around the Ring of Brodgar, with Zear and Aether located by the Stone of Destiny in the centre of the Ring. It was a cloudless night. The Milky Way shone bright. The key star Arcturus was especially bright.

Zear addressed the devoted multitude, "Friends, you know us and what Aether and I stand for. The light and goodness. Our campaign goes well. Max and Airna will report back on the mainland on their return. Meantime, we thought it would be useful to take forward our mission. Please raise your right hands. We will need to call on the dormant light therein and imbued in the Stone. "

Aether and Zear then joined hands round the Stone, chanting in a strange tongue that none present had heard before. Slowly but deliberately, Shadows crept from both of them producing a conflagration of darkness encased in a seething maelstrom of corruption which garnered power as a shaft of it leaped skywards, heading for the stars.

A particular star – Arcturus – was the target and the dark flume reached there instantaneously and was deflected on to the whole greatness. The crowd was stunned.

All this was about control. Earth was just another plaything for the Watchers. Then the control fell like black snow. It fell over the entirety of the planet. Total control was now in place. The Watchers could play many games at any time. How jolly to have these humans available to be used at a whim. The Star Sisters would be rewarded.

Chapter 10
Betrayal

The crew of the *Light Bringer* woke up to a very strange vista. Everywhere there was a thin layer of what looked like black mercury. When you put your boot through it, it parted lugubriously as if reluctant to leave you. All were astonished, not knowing what to say or do.

Nigel said to Andy, "What next Andy. We have seen some damn queer sights my friend but this takes the biscuit. What in the name of the wee man is this gloop?

I don't know about you, but I am well past worrying about it. Let's just get through another day."

Airna turned to me and then to the crew, "Well friends. I feared this day would come. You have all had a great deal to adjust to, not least the magic. Now, with this latest development, there is a need to let you know just how strange all of this is and how much stranger it could get. Penumbra and Erebus have gone – they were on Earth to act on behalf of the Star Masters, who are alien beings, billions of miles out in space and hell bent on promoting evil.

"Aether, as you know, stood for the light and we followed her without hesitation, convinced of her cause. The sad news dear friends is that Aether was always on the dark side. But she had been, for most of her life, under the Shadow and controlled by Zear and the Seeker. Together, and on behalf of the Star Sisters, they plotted to defeat Penumbra and complete their mission – to control all living things on this planet. The Star Sisters are a much darker force than the Star Masters."

The crew were dumfounded and astonished. All they had held dear now turned on its head. John then asked on behalf of the crew, "We understand what you say Airna, but who can we trust. Lives have been wholly committed, and indeed given, to the unicorn cause. We stand for good and will die for that end. Our planet has now gone from one calamity to another. Just as the climate reversal was beginning, and the light was shining through, this weird event has happened.

Hard to comprehend. Hard to believe. But there it is – we feel it's potential malice. Reassure us Airna if you can."

"There is a great deal we can do and you must now trust me. But I need to explain more now so you have the whole picture. The black gloop will abate quickly. However, it will secure a Shadow to everyone who will then be controlled by the Watchers.

Now, the Watchers control all the magical people you have encountered so far. But they do not control me. Strange as it may seem, the Watchers will use us as we used games on our PlayStation. They may never control you but could do so at any given moment, at a whim. Our mission now, with myself in the lead, is to reverse this process and remove this planet permanently from their game board. And the good news is that I can do that, with your help."

John pressed on, "But it was your mother who caused all this. You ask a lot of us Airna. You yourself are like them, possessing strange powers and coming from who knows where. And Max, you are Airna's father. Are you both now manipulating us to your nefarious ends."

I understood just where he was coming from. Our credibility was suspect, so I suggested, "You are right. Why should you trust and follow us? Because we are all you have. Without Airna there is no way back. It's as simple as that."

The Duke was not letting this go, "I hear you Airna. But I too am finding great difficulty in accepting the duplicity involved. I, for one, believed implicitly in your mother's honour and her dedication to goodness."

As the sun set, all the black covering had gone. Except, all save Airna, now had a suggestion of Shadow within them. Indeed, they soon noticed the fluctuating shimmer around colleagues. Deeply troubling. Like someone being inside you. Ghastly. It would, in time, drive many insane. Some slept that night. Most didn't.

Airna discussed strategy with Max throughout the early hours. The Duke was not consulted. A Meet took place after Nigel served an excellent breakfast. There was much confusion, concern, uncertainty, doubt and deep seated fear.

Airna took control, "To put this right, we need to return to New

Orkney and the Ring. It is there, in the Ring, that you find the star control. That is where I have to get to free all of you from a dire fate. It will not be easy. But I am above all who have gone before me. I truly am star light incarnate and am here for this very purpose.

"I am the Star Born. You will all see what I am capable of. We rest today, ready the ship tomorrow and set sail for the north tomorrow evening. I understand you play the bagpipes Andy and Bethsheba the accordion – tonight we sing and dance."

And so it was. A splendid starlit night that proceeded without incident and was loved by all. Andy certainly knew how to play pipes. Soon they were casting their spell. The slow pibroch was haunting and ethereal. The jig joyful and uplifting. The impact on the listener is magical, somehow getting into your inner self and your soul.

Deeply moving and you are not sure why. There are no pauses and that may hold some of the secret. The accompanying accordion added to the beat and the fun. The crew danced the night away, aided by a generous measure of whisky.

All were a bit groggy in the morning. But all the signs were that they were ready to go and head for Orkney. It would be a long and difficult passage and going ashore would be necessary to reprovision, not least for fresh water. There was a fresh south westerly and the sails, with topgallants set, were full and *Light Bringer* was leaping forth at some knots. She was as sound as the first day she took to the water.

Sailed like a small boat and, like some fair women of adventurous life famous in history, seemed to have the secret of perpetual youth. As such, there was nothing unnatural in Captain Tatters treating her like a lover. A ship can be a symbol. If thought of as isolated in the midst of the ocean, a ship can stand for mankind and human society moving through time and struggling with its destiny. How true that was of *Light Bringer* and all who sailed in her.

The crew often took the opportunity, when becalmed, to dive overboard and swim. Most mariners were excellent swimmers, but Andy the Gun was a very poor swimmer. And he was teased mercilessly. Bethsheba swam like a fish and could hold her breath for prodigious lengths. Diving in the ocean is a sense of being at one with nature, to a place that tells to the beginning of creation.

For some, the sea salt water was their freedom, a release from the everyday rules of gravity and a chance to experience weight-lessness. Looking out to sea, the ocean stretched out, a seemingly eternal expanse of azure blue that merged with the sky on the distant horizon.

The water's surface shimmered in the sunlight, like a million tiny diamonds dancing on liquid glass. A vast mirror like calmness enveloped the ocean, creating an illusion of stillness that seemed to stretch into eternity. The horizon was a seamless blend of sea and sky, as though the world had been painted with gentle strokes of blue.

A far cry indeed from the black snow.

Then the weather changed, the ocean such a fickle unpredictable beast – one moment captivating with its vast limitless beauty, the next threatening your very existence. What a wild creation it was. Dark clouds gathered on the horizon, casting ominous shadows across the ocean's surface. The sea, stirred by unseen forces, became a canvas of oncoming danger as the waves began to rise into angry titans.

Waves and sharp hot rain lashed and seethed against the ship, engulfing the deck with floods of frothing water. Shouts cried out but the deafening thunder drowned them out with every crash. The mast vibrated but held firm as the sails were reefed and furled. The waves beat and punched the ship with all of their might and the wind gusts knifed the rigging, testing every timber. A storm such as this brings a quickening sense of perspective and the relative size of the ship to the brine.

Lightning cracked the sky sending shards of light through the dark sky. An immense dazzling guillotine blade of lightening streaked across the night sky, illuminating it with a stark blue whiteness and flooding the ship. A funnel cloud snaked its way towards us like an inky black finger.

The thunder struggled and howled in fits and starts, until it rumbled closer and closer, and cracked overhead. A gigantic bank of dark cloud massed above the ship, seemed to writhe and twist, growing and swelling as if it were alive.

The crew had seen it's like before. Soon the thunder was heard in the distance, the vicious wind eased off and the storm moved on like a dark monster. The pulse of the ocean was now steady and peaceful.

The hours dissolved into each other as I watched the sky fade from black, to grey, to baby blue and then to a dim aqua dotted with flurries of light clouds. The blue was soon replaced with a dazzling saffron as the sun sank deeper into the horizon. The ship had, by now, settled into a steady comforting rhythm after the storm.

Later on that evening, my eyes were greeted by the vast multitude of glimmering stars that illuminated the charcoal sky. It was this still sight that allowed me to finally accept that the storm had well and truly subsided. Only then could I slip into the grip of sound sleep.

True adventure, unlike it's packaged and tamed cousin, means embarking on something without having an assured outcome. That is what we were on together. How we thought, acted and worked together would affect the outcome.

Tatters sidled up beside me, "Sailing a ship through a storm is like dancing with nature in its rawest form. Truly invigorating. Only then, when faced with it's might, do I feel truly alive. To set the sail's right and to steer the correct course is sheer joy. Let us sail."

"We are indeed fortunate to have you with us. Much lies ahead. Our team will be tested. "

The ship demanded constant maintenance. Not least the sails which were complex and constructed with considerable skill. To function well, a sail needed to be strong enough to withstand the power of wind and battle damage but also light and flexible enough to be handled by sailors working aloft, often in challenging dangerous conditions.

This balance was difficult to achieve because the stronger the type of material used, the heavier and more rigid the sail became. The solution was to use varying grades of canvas in different parts of the sail, with lighter material in the centre, and heavier canvas towards the leech – side edges – where the most strain occurred.

At the edges of the sail, the canvas was doubled over to

increase its strength and then a bolt rope stitched to the edge to prevent it splitting. The rope was offset so that, even on the blackest night, a sailor could distinguish front of sail from back by touch alone. The sail then needed to have various holes, reinforcement points and sail reduction ropes.

The days passed at sea, with everyone allocated to the tasks that had to be done. Fresh food and water would be needed in the next day or so and the decision was made to head for shore and a harbour that could take their draught. Catterline, a small fishing village on the east coast, was identified as a possible port of call. Entering unfamiliar harbours can be difficult and stressful, with plenty of scope for getting things wrong.

Tatters knew exactly the ship's characteristics, the level of experience of his excellent crew and the extent of his knowledge as a skipper. The first step was to share the planning with the crew, motivate and involve them, let them know what is going to happen, equip them to take action and to cover for any mistakes made.

Charts had to be read and studied and safe to navigate waters identified. Then there were tidal streams, the state of the sea and anchorage details. As well as a fall back plan which included alternative harbours, anchorages, tidal streams and depth data.

Two days passed, and on the morning of the third day, our planned destination came into view. The sea was set calm, with a soft floating breeze. Mooring lines and fenders were readied. And the small harbour approached.

Just then, the Watchers decided to intervene. The harbour entrance was treacherous, with jagged rocks waiting for the unwary mariner. The crew were slowing their ship down, furling the sails, when the *Light Bringer* lurched rapidly towards the needle sharp islands either side of the harbour entrance. The sailors then found the Shadow upon them, rendering them unable to save the situation.

Airna had been sleeping and rushed up on deck to see what was going on. But she was too late. The *Light Bringer* started to roll from side to side. All aboard grabbed what they could. The lighters were lowered ready to take all who survived ashore. The temperature dipped all of a sudden and dark clouds obscured the moon. Heavy rain rushed towards the ship like a wraith's veil of sorrow.

The ship heaved and ground on the rocks, straining to get loose from their death grip. Tatters was standing erect at the tiller hoping, straining every muscle and was totally stricken. He could just make out the figure of a man standing on the shingle beach, lamp raised aloft.

Then it disappeared as the cloaked sky blotted out the light of the moon. The rain whipped down like crystal nails. The sea swells rose and sped the ship to her doom. The ship bobbed like a cork and keeled and tilted like the death flop of a fish. The timber planks buckled and bulged, then screeched and shuddered, but she righted herself.

Tatter's two hands gripped the tiller, refusing to let go. His father's words came back to him unbidden, "A true mariner never deserts a sinking ship."

He gripped on tighter. A mountainous wave rose up before him, blotting out the sky. The wind howled out his doom. The boat rose with the swell, inclining upwards to her destruction. She was propelled up on to the razor sharp edges of the outcrop, hovered, and her superstructure was pummelled into small fragments of splintered wood. Then she went down into the depths swallowed whole in a final, terrible, squeak and moan of sundered timber.

In just minutes all was lost. Most of the crew had managed to deploy skiffs before the ship broke apart and had headed away from the spreading wreckage. There was nothing but floating debris where the ship had been.

Lorraine, the archer, was unable to hold on to anything and was washed from the deck into the sea just before the ship broke apart. Fortunately, she was a good swimmer and struck out for the shore holding her beloved bow as clear of the water as she could, heading steadily for the skiffs and the foreshore.

The skiffs made good headway and the crews, pulling strongly against the rip tide, propelled their craft on to the shingle beach. All were in a state of profound shock. I wondered how much more we could take. Airna was angry and concerned, counting those present. Lorraine and Tatters were missing.

Within minutes an exhausted Lorraine beached rather inelegantly on the beach, holding her bow Darling above her head. There was a triumphant yet grateful look in her searching green eyes. She had survived to enjoy her craft. Had the water been deeper and she shorter, it is doubtful that, even as a competent swimmer, her stumbling attempts to stay afloat would have kept her alive.

All were drenched but not cold – the sea was very warm, almost too warm. A motley group stood further up the shingle, looking suspiciously at this strange gathering on their beach. They did not move, holding their lanterns aloft.

I strode towards them, the shingle crunching under my soggy

boots. Their leader, a tall thin man with a black beard and smoking a pipe, sauntered towards me. I noted his over-confident strut and the revolver in a holster at his side and only hoped that Airna had seen it to and would guard my back in the event of any trouble.

He spoke. What a cadence. Spoke doesn't really cover it: he addressed me more as if I were one of his servants, charmingly yet dismissively and with supreme self-confidence, "Welcome. I hope so. We are in hard times. Forgive the absence of hospitality. Care is the watch word. So, strangers, come with us and get some food and dry off."

I was very, very, wary of this gentlemen who had the touch of the dark about him. Used to getting his own way. He would be cruel and ruthless should it be called on. We needed to, first, get a sense of the strength he brought to any fight should it come to that. And we had to assess what this small rural hamlet had to offer our quest.

It looked as if our brave captain had gone down with his dear companion, the *Light Bringer*. So, we all gathered the little we had left and, together, plodded up the beach fully alert and still armed. Sadly, we only had the ammunition we had in belts round us and getting more would be vital. Meantime, we were vulnerable.

We ascended steep cliffs and I could just make out a row of white cottages spread along the edge like a stiff collar. Lanterns were being lit and they shone like white diamonds blurred by the lashing rain. On cramming into the old inn, hard faces scrutinised us with hostility and some fear. We were quite a daunting group, bedraggled and armed to the teeth.

Airna moved to the centre of the smoke filled room and addressed the host, "Friends, and I hope you are our friends, I am the leader of our small band and want to thank you and all in your community for your warm welcome. Do not fear us. We do not want to burden you and do not intend to stay more than a day or two. Our situation is difficult but we have many skills and, whilst with you, can contribute."

Their leader had been seated. Standing, and drawing his black cloak around him, he looked around him saying, "These are fine words. But we have little food in this strange world we seek to survive in. You are welcome but, you are right, we really cannot sustain your crew for more than a couple of days. You clearly are a very sophisticated fighting unit. Please do not assume we are without arms or unable to resist. Meantime, rest assured we will do all we can to host and send you refreshed on your way."

Airna responded, "Very gracious. My name is Airna and our crew will soon get to know you all. You will want to know about us. Well, we are heading north to the northernmost islands of Caledonia. Now without our dear ship *Light Bringer*. Our brave captain appears to have gone down with her, a true mariner to the very last."

We all settled into the upstairs of the inn for the night. Although exhausted, guards were set. Now would have been the time for a surprise attack so Airna stayed fully awake, patrolling the inn grounds.

The Duke took his chance to get in a word with Airna, "I sense turmoil here. Something is not right. Be careful. They are a treacherous lot."

"Yes, dear Duke. Darkness resonates. Deception lingers. I am ahead of it. Rest assured."

The night, thankfully, went quietly without incident. A new day broke and Nigel somehow orchestrated a meal for all, having already got to know the inn staff. Day broke with warm fingers spread across a dawn sky. They grew, tentatively eating away at the dark, becoming more and more until the traces of stars disappeared, blinking away in the stark reality of morning.

The burnt grass on the top of the cliffs shimmered, thin tendrils of dust dissipating into the mist. A flock of hungry birds became commas above, taking wing briskly and breaking the flat, open tundra of the sky. Patches of sunshine advanced toward the scree slopes on the vertiginous cliffs and on upwards, spreading like gold silk threads across the row of quaint cottage fronts.

That morning the crew explored the hamlet and the arable hinterland beyond, reporting back that evening on what they had established and who they had talked to. The community leader had a large comfortable lodge nestled amongst the fields set to the rear of the cottages. Surprisingly, he had a small herd of horses in good condition – a rare sight and much prized, not least as a mode of transport. There was also a barn next to the lodge.

That night, in the pitch dark, some members of the crew approached the barn taking great care. The barn was locked. Woody was adept with locks and quickly opened it, pocketing the iron fixing. A flint was struck and a torch lit. In the flickering light, they saw wooden crates.

One was prised open and there, in glittering array, were rows of bullets. What a find. The issue now was whether to take all the crates and the horses or, in fairness, settle the account. We had the means. Bethsheba, and two other members of the crew, had bullion belts filled with gold pieces. The top of the crate and the barn lock were restored very carefully.

Very early in the morning Airna and I considered the ethics of our dilemma, concluding that we would make a generous offer for half the horses in the herd and half the ammunition. Word was sent to their leader – called Red – who came to the inn. The proposal was put. The main problem being that, in so doing, they were admitting to breaching trust by breaking into his barn.

Red was disturbingly calm, welcoming his guests warmly. This would not go well. But it did. A settlement was reached and payment handed over. The horses, loaded with ammunition, would be ready to take away the next morning. Airna let the transaction proceed, all the while well aware that Red may well deceive them.

And so it proved. Next morning there was no transportation. However, we had had an eye on Red's team and observed them moving both the crates and the horses overnight to a cave at a cove at the foot of nearby cliffs. It was an easy task to overwhelm the guards. We went directly to confront Red, who told us point blank that he was keeping our gold and had no intention whatsoever to allow us a single horse or bullet. Airna smiled. Slowly, she explained the situation to a dumbstruck Red. He was fuming. His immense pride and pomposity punctured.

Airna addressed the population, "We stand for good and are on a mission to save this planet and it's future. You are all now well aware of the Shadow that captures us all. What you do not know is a great deal. I am the Star Born – behold the starlight I now cast over your heads. Those who wish may join our quest. It is a truly glorious one."

"As for you Red. You may keep our payment and we will take with us what we are due."

The next day the quest set forth from Catterline. Two worthy souls joined us. The horses would prove a real boon. The going would be gruelling, treacherous and many a battle was ahead of them. Orkney was a long way ahead. But spirits had picked up and they were convinced that the light would prevail. We had now to strike northwest round the massive Grampian plateau, heading eventually for Inverness, before then going up the east coast. With laden horses, and the ever present heat, we would do well to make twenty miles a day.

At that rate, it would be a few weeks before Orkney came into view. For the first week, all was normal getting into the efficient rhythm of making and breaking camp with all the laborious humdrum repetitive jobs that that entailed. Chores were shared, not least managing the privy. All got to know there two new companions – Judith a nurse and Archie a groom.

There were six horses with us, including Archie's favourite. Five were competent work horses – Thor, Tank, Maximus, Tinker Bell and Pirate. But one was a warm blood thoroughbred called Fire. A magnificent horse bred for stud and for speed. A bit more nervous and energetic than other equines. Needing care and attention.

We made good progress but we were noticed as we passed through the land, riven with competing bands of brigands looking for easy spoils. Our crates would make very rich pickings as would our horses and the gold we secreted out of sight. It was just a matter of time before we were attacked. As always, we set guards.

It was our second week out from Catterline and our dear captain and his precious *Light Bringer*. Camp had been set by a stream in a small steep sided glen just off the road. Andy was serenading the camp with his pipes and we were relaxing by the campfire. I thought I heard something.

An odd sound. Different. I raised my hand and motioned for silence. I got it. That second saved us. They had got far too close. Our guards must be dead. And then were upon us. That second allowed us to reach out for our weapons. We met the onslaught. And it was shattering. We formed a circle. The horses whinnied and stomped, their eyes white with terror.

Lorraine released arrows like confetti in all directions, some finding their mark, others embedded in shields. Our soldiers opened fire, finding one mark after another. There was some sporadic return fire. Then Andy sprayed bullets amongst them and took a heavy toll. The exchange was bloody.

Suddenly, dark figures were heading up the glen in retreat. We did not go after them. Two of our soldiers, on guard duty, were sadly dead having had their throats cut.

New guards were set. Morning came and having buried our comrades and struck camp, we moved out.

In the third week, we reached Inverness. Being a city, it was busy but we still drew attention as an especially well armed unit. No matter how much we played this down. Rumour was rife. What was this weird feeling everyone had. Where had the black snow come from. Would this strange world never end. But survival was all. Always looking for the deal. A way to make ends meet. To put food on the table. To live well. Familiar.

The unit set about recruiting. Looking for the willing, but even better if they brought specialist skills to the cause. Over the days, we had considerable success – ten new recruits. Nine young and one man in his seventies. But he was a farrier. Provisions were bought: as much as they could carry on their horses. Time came to leave and they could not tarry any longer. Best to move on and keep on moving.

The day they left was humid and wet. Insects bored and bloated. The horses were pin cushions. Still, there was optimism and a sense of progress as their platoon travelled north. The going didn't get any easier, tackling a river, burn or landslide. The coastline was peppered with deep, inaccessible valleys and cuttings but the roads, although tacky and sticky, afforded along their sides, a way ahead. Still, it was hard going in trying conditions.

There were still falls and accidents. One such incident was

when Lorraine was leading Fire across a swelling burn in torrent. The road had collapsed like many others swept away in the constant floods.

The water was putting tremendous pressure on them both. Fire was skittish and anxious and reared, pulling away from Lorraine who held on to the reins as Fire and her were swept down the cutting, heading for a severe waterfall drop into the sea. Andy rushed ahead, grabbing, on the way, a length of stout rope. It was not far from where they would fall over the waterfall. Just a couple of minutes. Andy scrambled down the scree, finding it hard to stay standing.

There had been steady heavy rain and the torrent was fiendish and rising fast. He saw Lorraine and Fire hurtling towards him. They would be in front of him in moments. The rope snaked out. Lorraine grabbed it and held on for dear life against the current, hell-bent on parting her from the rope.

Andy braced and hauled, his muscles strained to the limit. But together they did it and Lorraine reached the bank. Fire didn't. He was swept like debris over the waterfall, thudding from some one hundred feet into the sea. A great loss as he could have sired a new dynasty. Archie was inconsolable.

The next stop was the old fishing village of Brora. The lands of the Clearances and the House of Sutherland. It is said that Coineach Odhar, the Brahan Sear, prophesied that one day the Sutherland family would own only that land which could be seen from the windows of Dunrobin Castle.

It was late evening that we entered the village. All was quiet. We headed for the inn. And entered, under the low doorway, and were met with a sea of inquisitive faces, somewhat nonplussed by this strange procession of oddities now stood before them.

I seized the initiative, "Good folks of Brora. Fear us not. We travel north tomorrow and simply want to camp by the roadside to tonight and tomorrow night. We have a doctor and nurse with us should any require their help. And a farrier should you have horses to shoe. And if we can help in any other way let us know. We are headed for Orkney. "

A tall imposing figure strode confidently forward and shook my hand, looking me straight in the eye. He was every inch a God fearing man, with a white collar and black suit. Difficult to wear in the stifling heat. It required discipline and faith, "You are all welcome. God welcomes you. We have little to offer but do so with an open heart. Ours is yours whilst you abide with us."

We mixed and talked. As elsewhere, times were hard and loaded with deep superstition and mistrust. People had moved to the old faiths and beliefs as some sort of refuse from grim reality and the calamity at their door. The heat had been relentless, taking parents, grandparents and young children. Difficult to cope with. They could be led astray to the dark side as easily as to the light. Aether sensed dark in the inn. A deep cloying darkness.

Care was taken that night as we settled down on the roadside to sleep. Trust nobody in this troubled world. That was my axiom. The day dawned crisp and clear bringing with it new hopes and aspirations. There was a pearly glow in the sky. The dawn chorus of melodic bird song floated over the camp as if welcoming us.

Gradually, golden fingers of sunlight stretched across the village, bringing with it a flurry of early morning activity. Provisions were purloined and more established about their community comings and goings. They too were aware of how different they felt after the now notorious black snow affair. But all felt the village had a malice present.

Next day, the horses and mission fed and refreshed, and the camp struck, we readied to leave. But one of ours was missing. Andy had not appeared this morning, not seen since last night. The search began. No sign by midday. We were concerned. Enquiries were met with shrugs. Still nothing by evening.

Airna sensed impending doom. She was drawn to a steep valley cleft where the river Brora flowed down to the sea. Two armed soldiers accompanied her. They saw the smoke and smelled the heat before they saw it. A huge, banked pile of faggots and brush and, tied to a pole above it all, was Andy. A sacrifice.

This was enough for Airna. She strode up blazing with white light and, lifting her hand, severed the cords round Andy and then turned to the mob, "You know not what you do. These are rough times. Do not follow the dark. Resist the Shadow. I am the Star Born and I will save you all. Now leave. We will be gone in the next hour. The light will prevail."

We looked back on Brora. This is what the Watchers wanted and what delighted them. It added a sharpness to their lurid machinations. Such manipulation would not stand.

The heat and humidity, combined with the hungry growing insect colonies, was a deadly trio, inflicting pain and misery day in and day out. John, our doctor and Judith our nurse, were kept busy. Doing all they could with the limited supplies available. We made good progress though, having to traverse some tricky gorges where the road had collapsed into the abyss. But morale was good and held up well.

This northeast corner was very sparsely populated. On reaching the small fishing village of Helmsdale, we dispatched groups to gather intelligence and barter for food. The river there had a good run of fish and fresh salmon, were it still available, would be a welcome treat.

The port was busy, the small population going about their business. We were welcomed but few strangers came this way, especially from the roiling south. So, understandably, they were suspicious. Once again, being heavily armed, did not help our cause.

Unusually, no leader approached us. They just seemed content to barter and let us go on our way. And so it proved. After we enjoyed a signature evening meal of fresh fish skilfully concocted by our cook Gavin, washed down with whisky, we bedded down and got some much needed rest.

Early next morning we left our camp at the riverside, moving steadily north once again. The horses were bearing up well in the difficult conditions and the farrier Greg was a great help to Archie. Maximus had shed a shoe some furloughs before Brora and Greg had removed the old shoe, trimmed the hoof, measured a new shoe to fit, bent and heated the shoe to the proper shape and then nailed the new shoe to the underside of the hoof. In his element and glad to contribute. His skill could be important in building a future.

Periodically, the platoon would halt midday and spend the afternoon doing target practice. It was competitive. Lorraine loved to rile the shooters, goading them into competition. As usual, the aim was to see who could score the most, taking three shots at the butt placed one hundred yards out.

Andy, who was our machine gunner, was also handy at pistol shooting. He stood up to the range first, settled, assessed wind speed and direction, then aimed and fired three shots in quick succession. He scored twenty seven out of thirty. Impressive. Other shooters participated but were unable to do any better.

Lorraine came forward. Regal, poised, oozing quiet authority. Her leather arm guard was on her bow arm and she had a leather chest guard, all to protect against harm from the string and possible deflection. She used a bow with no sight or aiming devices, a barebow. As a skilled craftsperson, Lorraine not only crafted her beloved bow Darling but also her arrows. It was a skilled task and she was one of the very best at it.

The feather fletchings were made from the wing pointer feathers of a turkey. The pointer feathers have natural curvature distinct to the left and right wings of the turkey. She sighted, drew back Darling to its full torque, held the tension and released. Unlike a bullet, the arrow flew in a small arc, landing with a satisfying thud. Two more followed. Score twenty nine.

She had won once again. Woody, our carpenter, showed considerable interest in her craft and, truth be told, in Lorraine. They were ofttimes spotted chatting together. Many thought Woody was well out of his depth. I was not so sure.

The days passed in hard work and travel. The insects were unrelenting. The heat insufferable. Stifling. The flow lands were coming up. The insect life seemed to sense this, gathering in great columns and swirling overhead like some kind of avenging presence. It did not auger well. We entered the flow lands that night, setting up camp on the roadside.

It was hard going with the mosquitoes hell-bent on syphoning as much blood as possible. Some say that insects seem more intelligent and emotionally complex than they are given credit for. The way they marshalled their forces suggested to me that they could well have pretty advanced thought patterns and this new super-hot world was turbocharging their evolution.

The camp settled down for the night. They knew the threat that may lurk nearby. Extra guards were set. Any sleep was troubled. The heat was oppressive, extremely hot, unpleasant and difficult to bear. All had the consciousness of oncoming death.

As night settled over the bogland, there was a deafening chorus of life – frogs croaked, insects buzzing and whirring, grunts bleats snorts and wheezes from deer, the hoot from owls and some very odd glooping sounds, followed by silence.

And it was a strange silence that spread across the bog as night crept on sneakers quietly into the dawn. Morning came like a welcoming hand, inviting the good dreams of night to enter the day. I could smell the bog as I left my makeshift tent, hanging like a sour tangy perfume in the air.

Soporific, intoxicating and seductive. As if the murky pools were casting a spell to lure you in. Then, a cry of anguish. From Archie. Thor, the dappled mare, had gone. Like a thief in the night, the bog monster had struck. Avoiding more direct damage as if aware of the presence of Airna and fearing her powers.

Now down to four horses, the troop divided the load – mainly ammunition – amongst themselves. Several days passed by uneventfully before they reached Scrabster where they would, hopefully, commission a boat to take them across the Pentland Firth.

A torrid stretch of sea, acting like a boxing referee between two heavyweights – the massive Atlantic Ocean and the North Sea. Both now super charged with the climate disaster, broiling and roiling with intense heat.

Scrabster had a deep water harbour and was a gateway to our destination of Orkney. It dated back to Viking times. As in Catterline and Brora, and of course whilst on the now shipwrecked *Light Bringer*, the smell of the sea was intoxicating. An unmistakable mix of salt, seaweed and iodine. A mixture that embraced your clothes and, for some, their very soul.

It hinted at danger and adventure. We entered the village discretely, but as always, to little avail as the local worthies eyed us up and spread the word. By the time we found a campsite at the harbour, small crowds were gathered to find out who we were, why we were there and where were we going. Airna and I encouraged mixing, sharing some basic information with the locals and to find out, if possible, whether any boats were available.

That evening, at camp with our shelters set, we chewed over what we had been told. Best news was that there was a boat available. Andy our gunner and some of our crew had spent their evening in the local inn – Harbour John's. The boat captain was there. A giant of a man, hard and surly, not given to chit chat and who went by the name of Pooly.

His eyes were close set and he stank. But he did provide passages over to Orkney. At a price. And it was clear he saw us as easy and very gullible punters from the south. In these critical times, all were on the lookout for what they could get and we had arms and ammunition.

Negotiations were entered into with Pooly. He was evasive, elusive and difficult to pin down. He needed to be closely watched and Lorraine and her archers had that job. We couldn't help but suspect that Pooly was prevaricating to give him time to assess our weaknesses and plan an attack. And, once again, greed won out. Right in the middle of our fourth night, the horses whinnied.

They knew. Seconds later, the full might of the onslaught hit us. There were some shots fired and I saw one of ours fall as if felled. Andy had his machine gun at his hip and was releasing sporadic targeted bursts to winnow out the considerable numbers of the enemy rushing towards us along the pier, stumbling over hawsers and bollards in the dark and falling to the rhythm of Andy's gun.

They stuttered but many still rushed on like dervishes, intent on destroying the interlopers. Some even came from below the harbour's waters, climbing up the ladders and striking from the rear. We stood firm, discharging our pistols. Bethsheba performed a dance of death, her rapier easing in and out flesh and leaving carnage around her.

I released my trusty sword, Honour Light, from its scabbard, swung to and fro countering strikes and thrusts. They were good and determined. Fish boxes had been upturned in the melee and the surface was very slippery, very dangerous at any time but deadly in hand to hand combat. One slip and a dagger met your throat.

The fight raged on with casualties on both sides. It was taking a heavy toll. Airna had seen enough. The raging captain Pooly rushed towards her, screeching expletives. That was the last he saw of this world as Airna heaved her dirk up through his throat twisting it until he fell backwards with a look of sheer astonishment on his grizzly face. His supporters faltered. Airna quickly eviscerated two more. That did it. They broke, retreating into accompanying buildings at the pier side. Looking round, I saw a sad scene.

Many dead and wounded. Wailing and crying echoed across the harbour. What a waste. Always the same. Such was the state of our land and our people. In crisis, light and dark appeared to do ancient battle. And our world had never been in, or experienced, such absolute crisis.

We were stunned. Our doctor John went from body to body, assessing the extent of the damage and dispensing care or grace. In total, we lost six, with another two needing minor surgery for their wounds. Many locals had fallen. Many families were now without a father or mother. Exhausted guards were set and the rest of us embraced sleep. Morning came.

Nigel did us proud once again with a magnificent breakfast to set us on our way and get our aching muscles and hearts up ready for the day.

Our depleted crew took a lighter out to Pooly's craft and secured it, with our mariners taking charge surrounded by what they knew and loved. So much better for them than being on land. The sea beckoned to them: salt water in their veins.

It was a sturdy sailboat, fully rigged and ready to sail. They ferried the rest of us over throughout the day. The horses were hoisted by crane into the lower deck – through the hold and into slings which were set to allow the horses just to rest their hooves on the decking.

Woody, assisted by Lorraine and some of the mariners who had seen this done before, constructed what was needed whilst Archie and Greg comforted, fed and talked to them. Brave Fire and Thor had left us. But we still had Maximus, Tank, Tinker Bell and Pirate. All fine horses and friends that had served us well.

That night was spent on board. We were wary following the vicious attack. The night passed peacefully. The morning saw our ship, the *Pentland Flyer*, heading out of the harbour. Soon we were under full sail in a brisk north westerly breeze. Good steady progress was made, *Pentland Flyer* living up to her name, cresting and cleaving the waves like a true thoroughbred, a very fast ship in the right hands.

A ship that almost steered herself once you understood her ways and wiles. We no longer had our captain Tatters who, sadly, had gone down with his dear ship *Light Bringer* in the rocks off Catterline. But we had his bosun Rammer who was as good a seaman as there was around. And he knew how to command and get the best out a craft and the *Flyer* was his lady.

The unpredictable firth did not disappoint. Several leagues out, the crow's nest announced an oncoming squall. It looked fairly innocuous. It wasn't. Behind it lurked a massive waterspout, ploughing a fast moving furrow in the sea surface with its swirling spout reaching skywards. It was angry, super-heated and super charged. If it hit the boat just matchsticks would remain. Rammer was like a man possessed as he stood determined at the tiller, anticipating this gyrating monster and it's intended path.

His eyes were on stalks and his concentration fine-tuned. It reared like a cobra snake over our ship, ready to strike. Last second, it veered right, the wake almost engulfing us so huge and powerful was the spout. The crew settled down, heading out of the storm now upon us, using all their combined skills and experience.

We saw the Old Man Of Hoy in the distance, as we approached Orkney. A massive sea stack. Needle thin, hundreds of feet high and looking as if it would fall into the sea at any minute. Created, over eons, by the sea eroding the cliffs surrounding it.

Then we navigated up the easterly side of the island towards our planned destination at Finstown. All was going well as night fell. Our ship was drifting between two islands in a narrow straight. Not listed on the charts, four or five currents met here, forming a devastating whirlpool The Swilkie. This was a powerful one that demanded respect. The contradictory currents produced powerful vortices that could even pull down and sink a large boat.

The very edge of The Swilkie had caught the *Flyer* in its evil net, pulling inwards relentlessly and remorselessly. Like some bizarre giant spider weaving it's web. We were in trouble. It was pitch black. The Swilkie roared and churned in agitation. The deck cantilevered, the horses stomped, the crew lost their footing.

Quickly, all too quickly, the swirling side of this maelstrom seemed to lean over us, ready to swallow and devour. Airna was pulled out of deep sleep, stumbled on deck and realised instantly that only moments were left. She had the power and used it. The bow turned, making way up and out of the whirlpool to safety. The Watchers loved it. What a show. We sailed on, mooring off Finstown the next evening.

Chapter 11
The Shadow

All looked calm and normal as I gazed out at Finstown over the bulwarks, turning to my daughter

"It is good to be back, but we have already been wounded by The Watchers. Until you remove their control mechanism, the Shadow, we all are captive and subject to their whims and indulgences. That we should be a plaything for them is, frankly, disgusting. Sadly, impossible as it sounds, you know just how real it is and how deadly."

Airna smiled responding, "Yes father, I need to lift the Shadow. Careful assessment will be needed and Aether and the Seeker will play an important part. They are formidable. The Watchers, however, have no realisation of who I am. They are in for a shock. They are far from the ultimate power. I am here on behalf of the Entity."

And so the embarkation began. Special care had to be taken with the horses who were carefully released and made a fine sight swimming to the shore. With Archie and Greg swimming alongside shepherding them. A temporary camp was established on the foreshore and what resources they still possessed were listed before they eventually struck out for the main camp at the Ring. No doubt their arrival had already been notified to that camp which was not far away.

That evening, with the setting sun rays creeping over the hill to the west, all were in good fettle. Comrades had fallen: they were alive. They finished off four whisky bottles they had managed to grab and bring ashore as the *Light Bringer* sank.

Strange what our priorities can be when facing imminent death. It was certainly appreciated now. We gathered in groups, laughing and joking. The flickering flames of our campfire with their bright warm glow beckoned us to stay gathered round, sing songs, share stories and forget the new world around us.

A peaceful night followed. Morning came. My tongue felt like a piece of wood in my dry mouth. Nigel came to the rescue once again, with a masterful breakfast that lifted us out of our respective alcohol induced stupor. Slowly we struck camp and headed out west to the Ring of Brodgar.

Insect life had not diminished since our absence. At sea there is something of a very welcome reprieve from their unwelcome ministrations. But we were now at their mercy. The irritation was palpable.

Sooner than we remembered, the stupendous, imposing Ring was sighted. There was something about it. Like the many standing stones we had passed on our journeys, there was some deep seated power you sensed but which was redolent of your inner self and mankind's struggle to get to what we were, where we came from, what exactly was the universe and did we have any part in it.

We had all forgotten just how vast the camp site was, stretching over the horizon out of sight. You smelled it first, the unmistakable reek of human excrement. Not surprising given the voracious unrelenting heat and humidity, the significant population and the difficulty of maintaining personal hygiene.

It almost made you gag. Quite unsettling and a possible harbinger of what was yet to come. A welcome party met us, offering to help us with our loads and accompanying us towards the camp centre. Crowds lined up to see our homecoming, shouting encouragement and support.

The smell was getting worse as we penetrated the densely populated camp. And there was something about the people. Elusive but something not quite right. A resigned acceptance. A darkness.

Myself and Airna were ushered into a rather splendid high ceilinged building, the floor richly carpeted and, at the far end, a fire casting shadows on a throne like structure. Seated there was a shady character, seeming to shift shape. It was wrong. Fundamentally wrong.

Airna was on edge but strode forward, "We come back from our mission. Where is the unicorn Zear and my mother Aether and who are you? "

The strange figure lifted its head. Two completely white eyes met ours. They were soulless and wanting, filled with malice and totally corrupt. The voice was more of a dirge, dripping with deceit and terror.

"Welcome. Our camp is your camp. Wonderful Zear and beautiful Aether have left us. Never ever to return. They have other planets to visit. I am here to continue their good work. These are good people who just need a little education. Not all are fortunate enough to see the light and I can help them.

"My dear Airna, worry not that your mother has gone. You ask my name – why Airna, I am called Mal and let me now offer my condolences for the loss of your dear craft *Light Bringer* that now lies submerged at the bottom of Catterline Bay."

Airna was thinking furiously what had happened during their absence. Had this thing somehow killed Zear and Aether or was there more to this, "Thank you for your warm welcome. We will do all we can to aid your good cause. Much blood was spilled to get here. We do not want to shed more."

We left the tent, heading for the outskirts of the camp where we could establish our own discrete site further away from the masses, the stink and be in a more defensible location. Meantime, some of our platoon were out and about gathering information.

Once pitched, we settled for the evening, discussing events. As suspected, Zear and Aether had called down the black snow and, having completed their ultimate task, we now knew they had left the planet. Airna and I still had some difficulty in accepting such treacherous behaviour. Aether and her colleagues were even darker than Penumbra. Such orchestrated treachery and duplicity. Incredible. And how did this strange Mal know about the *Light Bringer*.

Airna turned to me, "Max, this is difficult. Clearly the Watchers have taken the view that the presence of the Shadow on our planet is not enough and have placed the evil Mal to oversee events, no doubt anticipating my return and wanting a stronger force to match me. That is why Mal was posing as representing the light, whilst he assessed our strengths and weaknesses before striking."

"I fear you are right daughter. But I do believe Aether was a reluctant agent for the dark side, subservient to the Seeker. She foresaw the Stone of Destiny as a way to punch through this stranglehold. Albeit, just for a moment. And that moment came when you were formed between us Airna. So do not think too ill of Aether."

All were unsettled in camp and very wary. If they were to be attacked, it would come quickly. Guards were set that night. No attack. Next day provisions were garnered and defence and attack strategies gone through. Eventually, it was determined that the best form of defence was attack. To wait could mean being overwhelmed by sheer numbers. There is little doubt the camp was under the thrall of Mal.

Sooner the better to strike, in the middle of that night. It was cloudy, moonless, starless, dark, dank, hot and all was quiet as the designated sections moved silently through the site, spreading out pincer like to eliminate their target – the evil beast. A camp this size was never silent. There was always somebody round and about. And so it proved. Unfortunately, innocent lives were lost as no warning of our approach could be allowed.

The noose closed gradually on our prize. Andy positioned his machine gun. When the noose was tight, he raked Mal's tent with rapid gunfire, shredding it, and everything in it to pieces in seconds. Silence fell.

Then it came, over and above the chaos of the camp, deep

throated laughter. Next, Mal elevated from the tent floor, looking down dispassionately in mild amusement. The relative powers of the dark and light would now be fully tested.

Airna shot up skywards, in a shimmer of starlight. Mal struck, a deep red cloud racing to envelop Airna. She cast that aside with a slight movement of her hand. Mal smiled. More was needed. The Watchers obliged.

Then Mal formed a giant red ball in front of him. It started to glow, before it shot like a missile for Airna who blocked it at the last minute, as she reeled in the sky with the tremendous impact and energy of the strike.

Furious Airna shouted, "Now meet your end. I will have no more of this."

Starlight shot from all parts of the sky, shooting through the clouds like silver darts, all grouping together whilst alighting on Airna's outstretched right hand. The enormous power now gathered in this tiny spot grew and grew as Airna incanted a verse in some unknown tongues. When at its culmination, the brightest shard of light ever seen burst forth decimating Mal. Who was no match for the Star Born.

Her troops cheered. No resistance came from the camp. They had had to look away but had the measure of what had happened and there was no way that the populace were going to turn against Airna who addressed all the next morning, "My friends, you witnessed last night's spectacle. The dark presence of Mal pretended to be for the light but was in fact quite the opposite, fully committed to the dark side and, like Aether and Zear, out to control this planet. They, in turn, were controlled by their Star Sisters.

And, ultimately, by the Watchers, who just look upon our planet as a plaything. I am the Star Born who is now amongst you again. My mission to lift the Shadow cast on all. I now look to you to aid me and my platoon to do just that."

Airna had to recover. Mal had tested her. The Watchers were playing a hard game. This is not the first time that she had been selected to restore the balance that the Eternal Court adhered to and as directed by the Entity. She was one of a very few members of a very special order.

Two weeks passed as the camp was smartened up, improving hygiene and overall efficiency. The camp responded well, as if coming out of a bad dream. Airna sensed the hour coming. The culmination of her purpose here on planet Earth. She would soon leave Max, her father, behind. A Meet had been called for that evening. A massive crowd was there, surrounding the Ring of Brodgar. An ancient star gatherer site, linked to beyond the known universe, via the bright star Arcturus.

Airna stood to the side of the Ring on a small promontory and prophesied "I am Star Born. This Ring, together with this Stone, enables me to rid your planet of the evil Shadow forever and also to speed up the reversal of climate change first set into motion by Penumbra. Behold."

Airna turned, descended from the hillock, and embraced me, "Father dear, I now go to another place. We may meet again. I leave your world in a better place. A world reborn, where all are free and unfettered, where there will be opportunity for regrowth with love and life and all that is wonderful on your planet. I will miss you. Goodness is all."

I was confused. "I will miss you dear Airna. Your mother would be very proud. I hope your light spreads wider. The dark is always waiting in the wings, wanting to be the main player."

Airna strode forth, ascending the Stone of Destiny, reaching her hands in supplication towards a sky filled with stars. Even in the velvet night there is the light of the stars. When we yearn for the light of the sun, there are stars that herald the light of dawn. It is always the light we crave. Otherwise, we would be creatures of the night scuttling and hiding from creatures imagined or real.

She drew her arms across her chest, her head bowed in supplication. All went quiet. The Stone began to pulsate, becoming a rich translucent white like some gigantic diamond. The Ring started to resonate softly at first, building methodically to a resounding vibrating crescendo, bright light beams bouncing from stone to stone of the Ring through the Stone at the centre.

It was stunning and truly magical. Airna then raised her arms, beseeching skywards and incanting a strange message. An almighty vertiginous column of white energy shot skywards to reach the very stars themselves. Then she was gone. All stood aghast. Dumbstruck. And aware that not only Airna had gone, so had the Shadow. A miracle. The crowd bowed their heads in recognition of what they had been given. The light had prevailed. At least on our planet. And so the great revival began as the planet started to cool down. There was a long way ahead but there was real hope. Planet Earth would no longer be at the mercy of The Watchers. They were lucky. Others elsewhere would not.

On her arrival, and now in another place, Airna summoned the Eternal Court who were pleased. The Entity was. Airna had much to do. The light must prevail.

Only light. Light was all. Airna saw her opportunity. It was possible to bring Max here. Just for a short time, otherwise he died here. She bowed to the Entity. Which acceded.

One moment I was returning from the Stone and reflecting on the departure of our beloved daughter and, the next, floating down a tunnel pulsating with light. My senses were different here in this strange place. A feeling of happy inertia, sensing the coming of a great revelation. Where was I. Was I dead.

My watch was going backwards then forwards at a remarkable rate. Contrary to my heart which had slowed down incredibly. Eventually, my feet found a solid base which was made of a material I had never seen before.

A large black orb was now floating in front of me. A faint outline of a figure was discernible within. The orb pulsed and seemed to be looking at me.

A being disgorged and entered my mind, "What is it that troubles you Max. You have done well. We can give you much. Riches without limit. Women. Men. Power. Sainthood. Miracles. End wars. Feed the hungry. Stop pain. Even live forever."

"There is one thing I would like to know but most of all I would like to go back to where you took me from, I asked in the hope that this thing would understand. I was more than a little scared.

"And what is that Max. Think very, very, carefully before you answer as you may not like what you find out."

"Well, this is all very odd. I know not where I am,"

"You, my dear Max, have come to us via Arcturus, one of our universal syphons. Let us just say you now abide in that space where you cannot go into the past and cannot go into the future. The key to the light.

"Humanity has forever looked to the stars and out and beyond to the limit of our known universe, wondering what dark matter and dark energy are and what lies beyond and where it ends.

"Dear Max. The eternal quest. All limited by the extent of your knowledge which, let me now advise you, is very primitive. Almost neanderthal. As there are, no doubt, those way beyond my knowledge boundaries."

"If I am to communicate with you, how do I address you?"

"Entity will suffice Max."

"How many humans come here?"

"None, excepting you Max. To begin to comprehend what the Greatness is, one needs to release all your preconceptions. Difficult. No time. No space. No dimension. No gravity. Just light and energy."

"I find such a bizarre concept quite impenetrable."

"Ah, not the light you experience Max. Think of it more as a philosophy. A way of living if you like. Not far removed from what you primitive humans regard as goodness."

"That is simple to understand but so difficult for some to realise."

"As you have found Max, goodness cannot be taken for

granted. It is the light energy that is the determining force that steers all there is or ever will be and we are it's custodians. The balance must be watched and the dark energy held in abeyance at all costs."

Suddenly, the Entity dissolved back into the orb and dissipated, leaving me somewhat bereft. What an encounter. I waited in the tunnel. Time passed. Or did it. Then Airna was right there in front of me.

"Father, I brought you here to see you again for the very last time. I hope your meet with the Entity helped in some simple way to unpick the profound nature of the Greatness. You need only know that goodness as you know it and interpret it, is all.

"You could say that good things are valued for their own sakes, or as means, valued for the sake of the means they promote. And that by fulfilling the best capacities that we have, by becoming the best we can be, that we make lives that are generally good for each other."

"It does lead me daughter to wonder who, in the end, defines what is good and actually whether that matters at all in the overall scheme of things."

"Exactly father. You are right to ask that. Because it gets to the heart of the Greatness. The light energy that binds is everything and it falls to my Court to ensure that that energy forever suppresses the dark energy. The quest of the good is the good itself. The well lived life is the well lived life. And the well living of life is what it is to live life well. I leave you now father."

I was back on earth by the Stones. All this had happened in a nano second and my presence, save in that scintilla of time, had not left the planet. I was not sure it had happened.

But I knew what was right and good and, together with my followers, I would do all I could to ensure that goodness prevailed in this new world. However, it was not an easy task.

The Shadow was now eliminated from our planet but all now hung on how quickly the global temperature reduced to tolerable levels. By the year 2110, the temperatures were moderating a smidgeon but only very gradually. The heat in Caledonia was still intense and everywhere to the south was still a cauldron. At this rate, it would be many, many years, eons, before it was even possible to access different parts of the world, let alone live in them.

If humanity survived at all, it would be many generations ahead. Years of uncertainty and terror. Indeed, probably tens of thousands of years to return anywhere near the pre-apocalypse population and the levels of provision these civilisations had developed and enjoyed. All gone in one twist of our climate. Just like the ice age and other historic natural catastrophic events.

Over the years, I had reinforced the need to live our lives in the new world to the betterment of all. Underscoring that together we would prevail embracing a common purpose by putting goodness at the heart of our campaign. Many had died to that end and we owed it to them and everyone else on this planet.

Such a difficult demanding environment was however ever vulnerable, constantly open to disruption and fragmentation. There were always individuals and organisations promoting their own agenda, many of the more powerful founded on belief systems. Organisations where the members were absolutist, intolerant of opposition and hell bent on specific agendas. Familiar.

One such cult flourished. Led by a messianic individual who proselytised the coming of a Saviour who would sort out all our problems. The cult was evangelical and had tapped in very successfully to the frail mental state of many, shaken to their very core by world events way beyond their wildest imaginings and all in their short lifetimes. A Saviour was something to pin your hopes on. Much more attractive for many than goodness.

The cult was gaining more and more followers. I was concerned. We had been here before. It made me reflect on whether it would ever be possible to establish and maintain a prophecy of goodness. The cult leader was called Nimbra, a slight woman who, at first sight, appeared unexceptional.

I needed a more forensic look and assessment. So, I attended one of her preachings where her true self materialised like a nuclear reaction. She was magnetic, spreading the word with complete conviction. No doubting her success. She was definitely not to be underestimated. But what was her agenda.

It didn't take long to find out. Her followers paraded in scarlet uniforms asking those they preached at to follow their Saviour lest they find themselves engulfed by the flames. It was only a matter of time before they started to identify any who were not with them were against them. We had been here before. Sadly.

So, began an all too familiar push for control. By now I foresaw goodness taking a back seat. Confrontation followed, whilst Nimbra progressively orchestrated a skilful play for her way forward. And she proved successful.

This new cult, now in the year 2115, was at its zenith. By then I was old and tired, having sat back for some time from active promotion of our ever diminishing cause. Reflecting sadly, I looked down at my gnarled hand covered in liver spots and the faint outline of a unicorn. Which had lain dormant for many years but was now throbbing. Slowly, and with foreboding, I pulled my weary body up from the table, walked a few paces across the floor, turned and looked in my full length mirror.

It was there all around me like a black shroud. The Shadow. The Watchers had returned. I had always known the stealth of the darkness, it's insidious potential and it's insatiable desire to return.

Then, suddenly, I projectile vomited over the mirror and grasped my chest which felt as if a truck had landed on it. I died on my knees. Gone to the light. The Watchers had tried to pull me to the dark but had failed. They did not like failure.

My dear dog Smidge, a collie, padded over to his master, lowered his head, sank his teeth in and shredded a chunk of flesh. Smidge had new Masters and the Watchers always wanted more.